THE DARING ADVENTURES OF HONORIA PORTER: VOLUME I

STEPHANIE K. CLEMENS

ADVENTURES IN INK

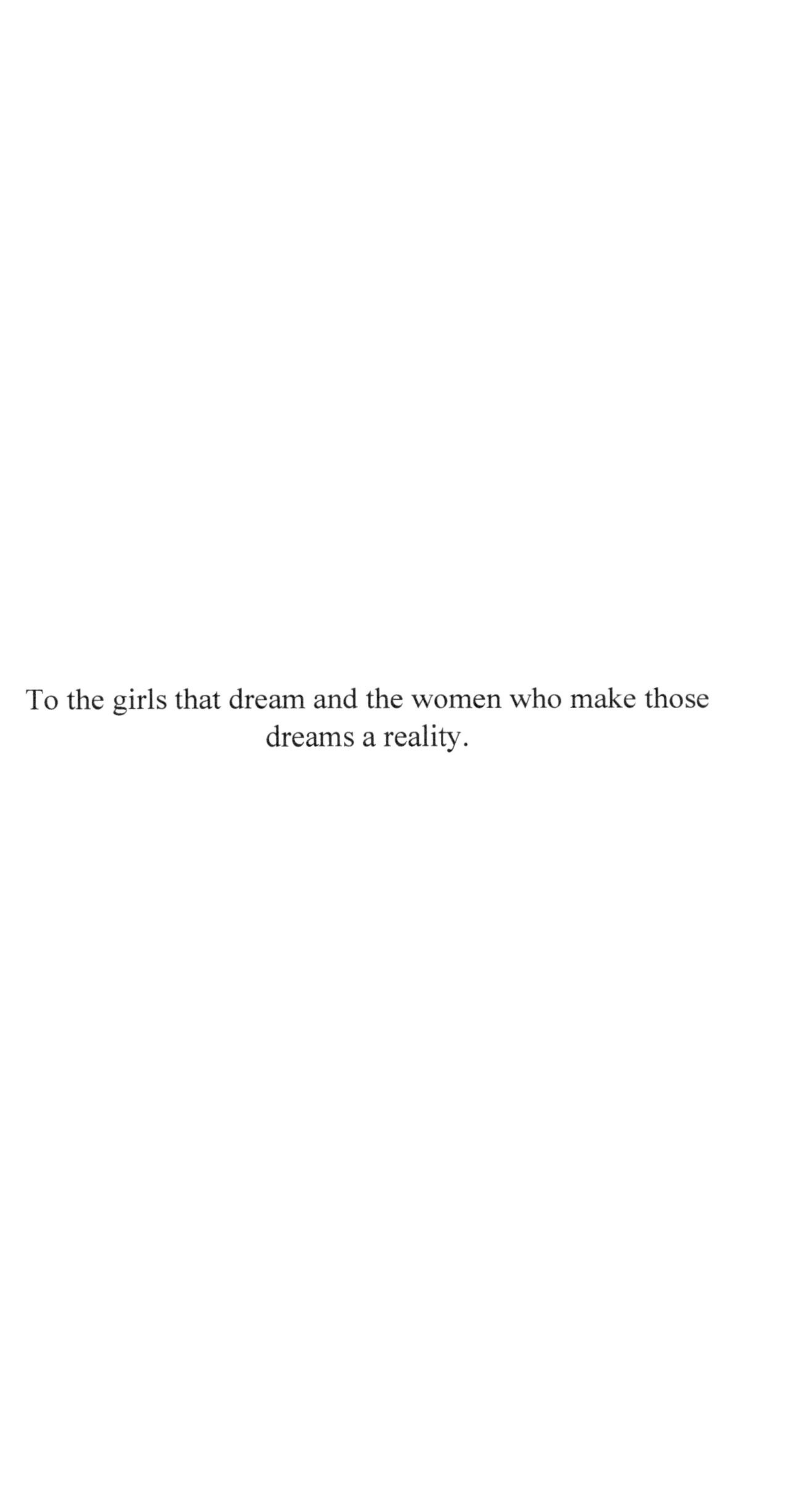

To the girls that dream and the women who make those dreams a reality.

The Daring Adventures

of

Honoria Porter:

Part One

The Crossing

Chapter One

Fintan, Brythion, June 12, 1850

Dear Diary,

Today started just as one would expect the day to start for a young lady in the midst of her third season. I called Lia to my room to help me dress for the morning. She is the perfect lady's maid for me. The two of us gossiped about the musical I attended the night before. How the Wentworth sisters believed they had more talent than they actually did. Cruel I know, but it wasn't very sporting of them to make us listen to their singing either. Then we moved on to who had spent time with whom on the balcony, or even more shocking, in an alcove, with the last few moments on how handsome the Duke of Farrington really was, and how lucky we young ladies are to have such a young and handsome duke looking for a wife this season. Not that I have any interest in being anyone's wife. But he is a fine specimen of a man to look at, and I wouldn't mind having a moment alone with him, as long as I didn't get caught.

Breakfast was the usual affair, with Mother going on about what events we were to attend today, and who she hoped stopped by with flowers. She is at her wit's end on why I haven't captured the attention of any gentlemen yet, although she did say there was still time, but not much. This is, after all, my third season and I am very nearly considered on the shelf. Which is true, and I would be devastated if capturing a gentleman had ever been my intention. I might want to experiment with one, but that's about it.

It wasn't until the end of the day, at the Harcastle Ball, that everything went awry.

*   *   *

Well, I had certainly mucked that up. Duke Farrington was handsome, and his full lips looked so inviting. I had only wanted to feel what it was like to kiss someone so handsome once in my life. Most of my friends were able to get away with a kiss at a ball. But not me. As soon as we walked into the alcove and Farrington slipped his arms around me, my mother was throwing open the curtains, exclaiming loudly that I was in there with Farrington.

"Bloody hell, Mother, will you please shut your mouth? You're causing a scene," I said, rolling my eyes at her histrionics. I did not want to deal with her in the best of circumstances, and this was not the best of circumstances for me. For my mother, I'm sure she was beyond pleased.

"Honoria, you are ruined. This must be set right at once." My mother paced in front of the duke and me, the melodrama she was acting out, drawing even more of a crowd than was necessary. Granted, I thought any crowd at all was more than necessary.

"Ahem." Duke Farrington cleared his throat. Oh, bloody hell. He was going to do exactly what my mother wanted.

"Don't do it, Farrington. Do not even think of it," I said before he could do anything.

"Miss Porter, it wouldn't be right if I didn't think about it," Farrington said, pushing his wavy brown hair out of his piercing-blue eyes. God, he was handsome.

"Farrington, no . . ." I raised my hand like that would actually stop him.

Instead, he grabbed it and fell to one knee. Bloody hell, this was not happening right now.

"Miss Porter, would you do me the honor . . ."

"Get up, Farrington, you know you don't want this," I hissed.

"That is, Miss Porter, I would very much like it if you would do me the honor of marrying me," he proposed. He didn't listen to a word I said. Ignored every word I had uttered and proposed.

"No." I ripped my hand from his and ran out of the ballroom, tears streaming down my cheeks, my red curls sticking to my face, as I ran away from the life everyone had planned out for me.

*   *   *

After hailing a hackney cab outside the ball—alone, courting even more scandal—I made my way up the stairs of our manor house, passing our butler and other servants as I did so. The shock on their faces transformed to concern as I made my way across the foyer. I'm sure I looked an absolute fright. My bright red hair was tumbling down my back, my hem wet and stained, and my silk slippers thrashed. I did my best to ignore them as I escaped to my room.

"Miss Porter, is there anything I can do for you?" our butler asked. I stopped midflight.

"Send Lia to my room. I need to change, and pack," I said, trying to catch my breath with my corset pinching my sides, limiting me to short and shallow breaths.

"Right away, miss."

I walked the rest of the way to my room, taking as deep of breaths as I could. Crossing the threshold into my room, my mood went from frantic to almost peaceful. Just being in a space that was my own calmed me. The blues of the walls, my paintings of ancient ruins like the Temple of Daelphine and the Library of Efiesious. Or at least paintings of drawings that I had seen at the Brythionite Museum. All I wanted was to visit one of these places in person and paint what I saw with my own eyes.

"Miss, do you want help getting ready for bed?" Lia asked.

"No, Lia, I need to change out of this gown into something sturdier, and I need to pack. I can't be here when my family gets home from the ball." It was all I could do to stand there as she unbuttoned all those ridiculous tiny buttons on the back of my dress.

"Finally," I sighed. "Not that you aren't efficient, Lia. Fashion today is just so fussy, I have no patience for it." I paced the length of my room and back again. "I'm going to need my green wool travel dress, a hat with a veil that covers most of my hair and eyes, and my sturdy boots. But before that, grab my valise. I need to pack."

I sat at my dressing table, gathering all of my jewelry

into a small case, then thought better of it. I would pin some of it to my corset and keep the rest in the case. I started to do just that, when I remembered my bank book, and my investments notebook. I would need both of those if I was going to get very far at all. My mother would be aghast if she knew I had been selling off certain pieces of jewelry for years and investing under a pseudonym—a male pseudonym that is. I had shares in the Sidhartta Trading Company, the Eletharis Transcontinental Railroad, a few different steel mills, and various other places. It might be time for the "Honorable Henry Porter" to sign over his assets to his loving niece. Unfortunately, that meant hiring someone to play her dear doting Uncle Henry, without letting the hired man know exactly what he was doing.

I let out an exasperated sigh. I was not leaving Fintan tonight. There was too much to be done before I could actually leave.

I needed somewhere to stay tonight. There was no way I was staying here. My mother would wear me down and have me married to Farrington by the end of the week if I stayed here. What a horrendous thought. Becoming property of yet another man, even a man that appeared nice, at least nice enough to kiss. Not that I had actually done that before my mother interrupted.

"Lia, I need a pen and paper. And a footman to deliver a note to Adelaide d'Argent."

Lia, the best lady's maid I had ever had, handed me the pen and paper almost immediately. I sat at my little white writing desk and jotted a quick note to Adelaide. I truly hoped she would take me in for a few nights without her parents knowing. This mad dash would be a complete waste if they handed me over to my family.

"What do you want packed in your valise, miss?" Lia asked.

"Everything that will fit. I don't plan on coming back here any time soon." I turned toward Lia, stopping her from working. "You could come with me, Lia. As my lady's maid or chaperone? I don't know if I can do this alone."

"Miss?" Lia's eyebrows drew together and her mouth turned down. I couldn't tell if she was confused or disappointed in me.

"I'm sorry, I shouldn't have asked that of you. For all I know you have a large family here, a beau, and wonderful friends who would be sad if you were to ever leave. I can't believe I was so inconsiderate."

"It's not that, miss. You haven't actually said anything about what's going on. I don't understand what's happening? Are you leaving, miss? And why are you leaving?" It would be a boon if Lia came with me, her speech was so clear and concise. She could easily pass as a well-to-do travel companion.

"I'm so sorry for my abruptness. You see, I was caught in a compromising position with Lord Farrington this evening. My mother was the one that caught us, and well, he proposed despite everything I said to prevent it. I'm ruined. I refuse to wed a man I don't know because we were alone for ten seconds. In fact, I have no intentions of ever marrying, and this just confirms it. I cannot believe my mother expected me to be manipulated so easily." I stood and started pacing again. I needed an outlet for all the nervous energy coursing through me. "Lia, I don't know if you have family here or anyone else to keep you here, but I would love to hire you as a companion. I plan to travel the world. I will see as much of it as I can, all the things I've painted, and more. Starting with Eletharis. I've heard the land is absolutely wild over there, as are some of the people. I've heard there are some places where women can even buy land. They still lose it when they marry, but can you imagine actually owning something for yourself?"

I sighed, throwing myself onto my bed and the pile of clothes Lia was trying to pack. Bloody hell, here I go messing everything up again.

"I'm sorry, Lia, there I go getting in the way again."

"You did nothing to apologize for, miss." Lia continued packing as I stood back up. "And miss, this trip you are going on sounds quite exhilarating. Are you sure you want me to join you? I'm nobody."

"Of course I want you to join me. I know I asked quite out of the blue, but we get along well enough, or so it seems. And it will give at least a tinge of propriety to the entire endeavor. We are both too young for it not to seem odd, but hopefully that will fade as we prove our competence."

A knock on the door had both of us freezing. *Please, don't let it be my mother. I have to be gone before she gets back.* I waved to Lia, encouraging her to answer the door. At my wave, she all but tiptoed over to the door, opening it just enough to see who was on the other side. Whoever it was must not have been a family member. Lia was handed a note. She quickly grabbed it and shut the door.

"It's from Miss Adelaide," Lia said.

I snatched it out of her hand. "Oh my, it seems my prayers have been answered and we have a place to go, if you will go with me?"

"I think I right will, miss. I'm keen for an adventure. I was lucky to get a job here, but can you imagine little ol' me traveling? It will be something."

"Go pack your valise then. I'll finish here. We need to be gone shortly." I shooed Lia off to her room, then got to business in mine: packing, hiding jewels in as many spots as possible, and finally grabbing my painting of the Library of Efiesious, before leaving my room forever and heading down to the servants' exit.

*   *   *

Chapter Two

Fintan, Brythion, June 13, 1850

Dear Diary,

Almost everyone I know would say that my life is in shambles. But for the first time in my life, I feel free. Like the chains of propriety have been unlocked, and I can move about the world in any way I choose. I'm probably overstating things, but I will savor this moment for as long as it lasts.

*   *   *

It seemed someone was looking out for me. The question was whether or not they were good, but either way, it made my escape possible. Lia and I had only walked around the corner when we found a hackney cab. The two of us sat in silence as the hackney drove away from my family home and to Adelaide's townhouse.

I couldn't believe I was actually doing this. I had wanted to pick up and leave for most of my life. And now, at the end of my third season, I was on the run.

"Miss, do you have a plan?" Lia asked interrupting my thoughts, twisting her hands over and over again.

"Oh, Lia, I can't believe you are trusting me enough to come with me. I do have an idea of a plan. First, I need access to my money. I've invested and profited over the last few years. But I did so pretending to invest as Henry Porter. I need to find a man to pretend to be my uncle or cousin or something, to sign over the accounts to me." I looked over at Lia; her wide eyes were almost all I could see in the dark carriage. "From there, I intend to book passage over to Eletharis. I want to explore as much of the country as possible. Then we can decide where to go next. I want to explore Junhar, Omazenas, Hellias, and maybe even Latika." I bounced in my seat, practically trembling with excitement.

"Why are we going to Eletharis first? From the painting in your room, I would guess we would be going to Hellias or Latika? You love all those stone places," Lia said.

"I'm assuming if anyone decides to look for me, that's exactly what they will think. They won't expect me to go to the new country first. Someplace with such an unexplored history. I would love to learn more about the indigenous people who settled the land long before anyone here thought to explore it."

"Yes, miss, I see. It makes so much sense if you don't want to be caught."

"Lia, you must get used to calling me by name. We are to be companions on this journey. I would like us to be friends, not employer-servant for the entire journey."

"Yes, Miss . . . Porter. I'll get there eventually, but it might take some time," Lia said.

"Very well, Lia. Hopefully, by the time we are on the boat over, you will feel more comfortable." I straightened my skirt, picking imaginary pieces of lint off it, doing everything I could to appear calm and in control. "Are you sure you want to go on this journey with me? I don't know when, if ever, I'll come back to Brythion. Of course, if you decide to come back, I'll purchase passage for you. But it could be awhile. Do you need to tell anyone you're going? I won't stop you from speaking to your family," I chattered on like a veritable nincompoop.

"No, Miss . . . Porter. Before going into service, I was

at an orphanage. No one is going to miss me at all."

"Oh, Lia, how did I not know this? You must think me terribly selfish to never have asked before. I'm so sorry." I felt like I had just put my foot in my mouth for the umpteenth time. My propensity to chatter on was always going to get me in trouble.

"Miss, I never wanted to draw attention to myself or my situation. It's not easy getting a job as an orphan. Too many employers see our status as somehow our own fault, and think it somehow affects our character." Lia folded her hands in her lap and looked up at me. It was like she was waiting for me to send her back.

I scrunched my nose as if I smelled something distasteful when in reality I was just thinking of other people's prejudices. "What balderdash. People are always out to believe the worst in others, especially when it comes to backgrounds they don't understand. If you had been born to a wealthy family, they never would have thought a thing about it." If I could pace in a hackney cab, I would have. Honestly, how do people sit still for such lengths of time?

I lurched forward as the carriage came to a halt. That's what I get for riding backward. I almost heard the driver's muffled voice as he made some inane announcement, presumably that we were at our destination.

Taking the initiative, I threw open the hackney door to see Adelaide's home before me, the red brick dull in the moonlight, much less welcoming than I remembered.

"Well, Lia, this is where it all begins. Let's gather our bags. Hopefully Adelaide is by the servants' entrance, ready to let us in." I looked back to see Lia directing the cabbie, a picture of efficiency as she insisted that he carefully set each bag down. His brow furrowed, but he complied. As he finished, I walked over, shoving a few notes into his now empty hands.

Grabbing two bags, I rolled my shoulders back, held my chin high, and walked resolutely towards the servant's entrance, counting on Lia to follow.

*   *   *

"Honoria, what in heavens has happened?" Adelaide asked, shooing Lia and me through the door. "You always have madcap plans, but this seems extreme even for you." Adelaide grabbed my arms, looking me up and down, her mouth pursed, her eyes etched with concern.

"Oh, Adelaide, you wouldn't believe it if I told you. But the time has come for me to leave Brython. If I stay, my mother will hound me into doing the unthinkable. And I just will not have it." Air whooshed out of my lungs. It might have been the most dramatic sigh of my life.

Adelaide took one of my bags in one hand and my hand in the other as she ushered Lia and me upstairs. She nodded to a maid as we came up to a set of double doors. Throwing open the doors, Adelaide gestured for us to come in. The room was astounding, decorated in emerald green and silver, almost the exact shade of my traveling gown.

"Oh, it's lovely, and Lia and I will be so comfortable here until we can book our passage." I wanted to flop onto the bed, especially after the night I had, but Adelaide looked about ready to jump out of her own skin. "Are you sure you are okay with this, Adelaide? I don't want to burden you."

"It's fine, Honoria." The constant wringing of her hands told a different story. I took her hands in mine, raising an eyebrow and cocking my head to the side. "Oh that, it has nothing to do with you. Marcus declared his intentions— Well, he told me of his intentions, and I want it more than ever. But after speaking to Corrine, I'm not so sure. Marcus is wonderful, but I don't know if he can offer me a stable future."

All I could do was stare. I might be against matrimony in general, but if someone I loved wanted to marry me, I would be hard pressed to turn him down. "I wouldn't listen to Corrine. She's looking for money and power and nothing else. You could have a wonderful life with Marcus, especially if you love one another. But I did just turn down a duke in front of an entire ballroom of people. Following my advice might be considered questionable at best."

"I wish I was as brave as you. I could never have turned down Duke Farrington. Especially with all those people around. And now you're off to have grand adventures on your terms." The sigh that escaped Adelaide told all anyone needed to know without a single word. I feared she was going to be trapped in a life she didn't really want because she was afraid to actually want something for herself.

"You could come, but I think you should stay and figure out a life with Marcus. I think that's where you will find your happiness." I didn't let her know I was terrified of the choices I was making. Even though they felt like the right choices, I wasn't sure they were. Either way, I was scared half to death.

"You're right, most likely. Enough of me. What are your plans?" Adelaide brushed invisible wrinkles from her gown as if she was brushing our conversation away.

"First, I need my 'uncle' Henry Porter to sign over control of my accounts to me. Which means I need to find someone to pretend to be my uncle. I was hoping we could convince Marcus to do it. But if that is too forward, I can find someone else. Then I'll book passage and make my way to Eletharis. I honestly cannot fathom what I will do once I'm there. But I'm wealthy, intelligent, and, well, I don't know what else, but I'm sure I can figure it out." I wondered how many times I was going to repeat my plan before executing it. I felt like I only had so many words at my disposal. Maybe that's why at some point I started pacing. I don't remember when. It was a habit of mine, especially when I was nervous.

"Honoria, come sit still. You are quite mad, but I'm sure you will make a success of it. Marcus is coming courting tomorrow. I'll ask him to help you out then. I would invite you down, but I think you'll cause quite the stir if you do. As well as get caught hiding out here."

*　　*　　*

Chapter Three

Fintan, Brythion, June 14, 1850

Dear Diary,

The world is an idiotic place. There I said it. I can't take it back now. I'm stuck in this room, a place I'm thankful for that is also my temporary prison, waiting to find out if there is someone that can withdraw my money for me.

It started a while ago. I would listen in at the study door in our home as father and his cronies talked business. They talked about the different stock markets, what to invest in, when to divest, etc. I would sit outside the door until they were done talking, then run up to my room and write it all down.

The next day, I would take half the pin money I received each month, the money I made selling some of my jewelry, and I invested it accordingly. I started this little scheme of mine when I was sixteen. Unbelievable, six years of saving and investing. And it had only improved once I was allowed to go to balls. All the talk I was able to listen in on, sometimes even encouraged. Some men do love the sound of their own voices. I have done quite well for myself.

The problem is, and why the world is stupid, no one would let me invest as Honoria Porter, so I made up an uncle, a male uncle of course, a Mr. Henry Porter, and now I need him to sign the accounts over to me so I can get out of this country.

Thankfully, Adelaide had a plan . . .

*   *   *

Lady Adelaide closed the door quietly behind her. Turning around with the loveliest smile on her face.

"Does this mean he will do it?" I asked, hoping her cheerful mood meant I was going to be granted access to my accounts.

Adelaide sat beside me on the bed. She always looked so proper. Something I had never been able to pull off. I blamed the red hair; it inspired my rebellious side.

"Of course he will. Marcus thinks you should go with

him. He wants to make sure that you have access to your funds, that there are no excuses later on from the bank. Isn't that sweet of him?" Adelaide said, all smiles and hearts in her eyes.

"It is very kind of him. I'll just have to go in disguise so my family doesn't find out I'm still here and who is hiding me." I definitely needed to cover my hair. It was the one thing that would give me away in an instant. No one else in society had hair even close to mine. "When are you going to tell Marcus that you're in love with him? You should, I think the two of you would have the most wonderful happily ever after."

"Did I just hear Honoria Porter talk about a happily ever after with a man? That has to be a first. You don't even believe in love and happily ever afters."

"That's not true. I believe in happily ever afters and following your heart. Which is exactly what I'm doing. I don't believe I'll marry for love. My heart yearns for adventure and excitement. My happily ever after lies on another path. I just know it. Unfortunately, the path is unclear. Let's hope it figures itself out here soon."

"I never understood your opposition to marriage, Honoria. I think being married and having a partner in life sounds wonderful." Adelaide lay back on the bed, eyes closed, clearly dreaming of her life married with a partner.

"I think it can be for the right man and woman. Like you and Marcus. I think the two of you would be so happy together. I do hope you tell him how you feel, Adelaide. You will miss out on so much if you turn your back on him."

"If I didn't know better, Honoria, I would say you're a romantic."

Little did Adelaide know how right she was. She just didn't understand the things I romanticized, like exploring places that had never been seen, finding artifacts that told stories of past peoples and their lives, basically anything and everything outside of Brythion and the restrictions of society.

*   *   *

I took my time the next morning, dressing with great care. I had put on my most severe-looking dress, a grey walking suit. Lia did my hair, pulling it back in a low chignon. It looked subdued even for my hair, but I feared I would still be quite recognizable.

"Lia, should I darken my hair? Or maybe I should dress as a widow. Something to cover up this–this beacon. I might as well wear a sign with my name on it." I sighed. No one else had red hair in my family, not even my sister Olivia, so I was the only redhead out this season. And by now, my scandalous behavior would be in every gossip rag there was, which meant everyone would recognize me.

"No, miss, dying your hair would be a shame. It mightn't look the same ever again. But maybe dressing in widow's weeds would be a good thing. No one likes to interact with a person they believe is grieving. It might also help during our travels."

"You are right, Lia. I wonder how long it would take to have a wardrobe of mourning clothes made for the trip? I'll have to see if Adelaide will go to the modiste for me. As for today, I'll cover as much of my hair as I can with that grey-and-blue bonnet over there."

I heard a gentle knock on the door in the pattern Adelaide and I had discussed. Before I could say a word, Lia had opened the door and Adelaide floated into the room.

"Marcus is waiting around the corner with a carriage. Are you ready, Honoria?" Adelaide smiled. I was lucky to have one friend that was this nice to me even when I was causing a scandal.

"I'm ready. I know I've asked too much already, and this might be too difficult. Do you think you can go to the modiste and order some mourning costumes? Maybe one black one to wear getting out of Fintan, and some grey and lavender costumes for half mourning for when I'm traveling. I have the funds, but I don't want to be seen." I looked up at

Adelaide, pleading with my eyes.

"I'll see what I can do."

I clapped my hands together, then hugged Adelaide with all my might. I hoped she followed her heart and lived a happy life. She was a person who deserved to be happy.

I followed her to where the carriage waited. Nothing about the carriage stood out. There was no coat of arms, but it looked nice and well maintained. Which is more than I could say about the hackney I had rented the other night.

"Thank you so much, Marcus. I couldn't do this without you. I hope you don't mind too much."

"It was bound to happen at some point. I just wish it was under better circumstances. Adelaide is going to miss your friendship," Marcus said, running his hand through his hair.

"I'm going to miss her too. Please look out for her for me. Why am I even asking? I know you'll do what you can." I hoped Adelaide had listened to what I said last night. The thought she would let society's rules push her away from someone who would support and love her towards someone else entirely terrified me. I wanted her to have her happily ever after.

I looked over at Marcus. He was handsome in his own way, unkempt and absentminded. But he was such a truly good person. Here he was, helping me out for no other reason than he was asked. How many people in this world were like that? I looked out the small window and as always, Fintan was grey, grey skies, grey buildings, grey everything. While the area I lived in everyone dressed in the colors of high fashion, it was not the case the further you got from the wealthier areas.

"There, that's the bank I've been using. I've been investing my money under the name Henry Porter. In their mind he is my uncle. Last time I checked, I had over five thousand pounds in the account. I would like to get out enough to travel to New Lankersham, and set up communication with banks in Eletharis, so I can withdraw money as needed, and if I'm very lucky, be able to set up deposits as well."

"You have always impressed me, Honoria. You have this all planned out. Even though it seems like a whim for you to run from here, I have a feeling these plans have been in the works for a while now. You've just never had a reason to actually leave before."

"You would not be wrong if you did indeed think that. Now let's go see what additional barriers they will find to prevent providing me with my funds."

Marcus knocked on the roof, alerting the driver we

were at our destination. He leapt from the carriage and offered me his hand, helping me step down with grace. I walked to the doors of the bank. The tall double doors were imposing, made from dark heavy wood with gilding around the edges. I squared my shoulders, preparing myself for the battle ahead, and pushed open the doors.

*   *   *

Chapter Four

Fintan, Brythion, June 21, 1850

Dear Diary,

A week has passed since Marcus and I went to the bank and set up my access to my own accounts. It was much easier than I had expected it to be based on the difficulty I had opening the account six years ago. The surprising issue had been booking my passage on the steamship to Eletharis. I had not believed that would be a problem at all. It took time to find a ship willing to take on two young women traveling without a male chaperone. I'm so glad Marcus had insisted on doing that after the bank, or I might be stuck here for some interminable amount of time in hiding. Being stuck in one hiding place is not one of my skills.

Adelaide had gone above and beyond and managed to get me clothing for the trip that would lend itself to a bit more respectable look. Some deep black widow's costumes, as well as some half-mourning costumes in shades of grey and lavender. She also had the foresight to find me some very petite men's suits I absolutely love and want to wear every day. I don't think anyone would ever believe me to be a man, my severe lack of height being the key problem. But I can see it helping in a pinch.

And now, Marcus and Adelaide were kind enough to take me to the docks so I could catch my steamship. I must admit, I am terrified at the prospect of leaving the only place I have ever known. But I am also so excited to truly start my daring adventures.

*   *   *

I said my goodbyes to Marcus and Adelaide, secretly wishing they would be caught together and forced to marry. Adelaide was too in her head about everything and listened to Lady Corinne way too often. I had said my piece to her many times during the past week I stayed there. I don't know if it had done any good. But there was nothing left for me to do. I would only meddle so much in someone else's life. Especially when mine was a bit of a mess.

I sighed, then pushed my shoulders back. Today I was dressed rather severely in a black silk gown with minimal trim on it. The gown covered almost every inch of skin from my neck to my feet, with the hoop and petticoats that held the skirt out covering my toes. I wore a dainty hat rather than a veil because I couldn't stand the idea of covering my face. I had limits to the charade I was willing to play.

I took a deep breath to steady the butterflies that were rioting in my stomach. Yes, undertaking these adventures made me extremely nervous. I may be leaving behind everything I knew, but it was my choice. I was choosing how I wanted to live my life, and very few women had that opportunity. Besides, I wasn't alone.

I looked over at Lia standing beside me, gazing up at the steamship wide-eyed and slack-jawed. She held her small valise in front of her. She looked every bit the travel companion a grieving widow would have with her. I was thankful for that. It was hopefully going to make passage much easier for me. I hoped she never came to regret going on this trip, a trip that might never end for me.

I started up the gangplank that led to the center of the ship. It was a long walk up, the ship's size an imposing reminder that my life was forever changing. At the top of the walkway stood the captain of the ship, or so I assumed from his decorated uniform and other members of the crew standing in a line beside him. Reaching the top of the ramp I stepped onto the steamship. The deck shifted under my feet, it felt as if the ground was suddenly further away. I stumbled into the captain. His hands slid around my waist, taking a second to set me right. I looked up and was instantly mesmerized by his stormy grey eyes. After a moment or maybe it was somewhat longer than just a moment, I stepped back with a small smile on my face.

"Excuse me, I wasn't expecting that." I looked up to study his face. He had a long straight nose, which sat above full lips that reminded me of Duke Farrington. I still couldn't believe my mother tried to trap me into marriage. I shook my head.

"It happens more often than you would think, especially if it's your first time on a ship. Feeling what you are used to being solid move beneath you can be quite unnerving. I hope it doesn't end up bothering you too much." He smiled as he spoke, causing fine lines to form around his eyes and a dimple to appear on his cheek. "I'm Captain John Castleberry. I'm here to make sure you have a pleasant and safe trip to New Lankersham. If you need anything, anything at all, myself or my crew will be happy to assist." He took my hand, and bowed over it. I felt like I was in the finest of ballrooms and not the entrance to a ship.

I took my hand back and walked away, ignoring the flutter in my chest. Well, almost ignoring it: I looked back. Captain Castleberry saw me and winked. I turned back, using all the willpower I had not to giggle like a young girl. One of the staff followed behind us for a moment.

"Ma'am, if you don't mind, I can show you to your cabin. It will be smaller than you are used to, I'm sure, but it is one of the nicer rooms on the ship," the attendant said as we walked. He stopped in front of the door towards the front of the ship. "Here you are, your cabin suite for the trip."

"Thank you, Mr. . . . I'm sorry. I don't actually know your name," I said.

"It's Mr. Jones, ma'am. I hope you enjoy your time on our ship. The captain has asked you to dine at his table tonight. Dinner is served at eight p.m.," he said, bowing slightly when he was done. Then he left with me still standing in the doorway.

I shook my head and turned to Lia. "Well, it is time for us to unpack. And then get ready for dinner. We are going to be at the captain's table tonight."

*   *   *

Chapter Five

Somewhere on the Ocean, June 21, 1850

Dear Diary,

It's hard to believe it, but I've actually left Brythion. So far, everyone has been very friendly, but I don't expect that to last forever. I'm sure the captain and his crew are nice to all the guests. And I did pay five pounds to have a pleasant room to share on the steamship with Lia. I had heard so many awful stories about getting seasick. I didn't want to be anywhere below deck where I couldn't easily access fresh air. The ship is already moving in a way my body isn't familiar with, and there is nowhere else to go for the next fourteen days. Lia and I will have to make the best of it and just hope that we don't get seasick.

The captain was kind enough to invite us to sit at his table for dinner. He is also quite handsome. His hair is mostly brown with blond streaks. I assume it is from being out in the sun on the ocean all the time. His smile, the dimple, and those fine lines around his eyes all go together in a very nice package. Anyway, it is time to get dressed. And I want to dress to impress.

*   *   *

I dressed in a deep-emerald gown, the skirt full and decorated with pink rosettes and gold beaded trim. I grabbed my emerald and diamond necklace, and with Lia's help, clasped it around my neck. Lia had donned a lovely bright-pink gown that set off her golden-brown hair perfectly and brought some color to her cheeks. I'm pretty sure she would look lovely in anything. If I had tried to wear that pink it would have looked horrendous on me, but on her—she looked perfect.

Together, Lia and I walked arm in arm to the dining chamber. The double doors opened for us thanks to two footmen. The opulence amazed me. I had not expected the ship's dining room to look like I was walking into the queen's ballroom. Gilded everything accented the ivory walls; the tables and chairs in contrast were made from mahogany and stained a rich dark color, and crystal chandeliers hung from the ceiling, swaying with the motion of the ship. The movement of the chandeliers with the flickering candles worried me. It looked like a fire hazard. However, no one else seemed to be worried. There had to be at least ten tables in the room, most of them already filled with people.

A member of the ship's crew escorted Lia and me toward the captain's table in the front of the room, and all eyes were drawn to us as we crossed the expanse of the room. Finally, we were brought to a table, the one I assumed was the captain's table. There were eight place settings at the table, and only two were empty.

"I'm sorry, Captain Castleberry. It appears that we are late for dinner," I said.

"Two beauties such as yourselves could never be late, for nothing can start until you enter the room." He took my hand and pressed a kiss on the back of it. He was a practiced flirt and the type of man that made me want to experience all the things young ladies were never told to think about. "Won't you have a seat?" Captain Castleberry gestured to the chair to his right. Apparently, I had left quite an impression on him.

There were five people at the table I didn't recognize. Three looked to be related. I would guess a mother, father, and daughter, making the gentleman on the daughter's left a suitor. Which only left the man sitting next to Lia. Honestly, I could not even think to guess who he was.

"Now that we are all here, let me introduce everyone. There is Mr. Arthur Wilcox, his wife Mrs. Violet Wilcox, and their daughter Miss Gwendolyn. Sitting next to Gwendolyn is Mr. Nelson Wright. He is in business with Mr. Wilcox. Next to your companion," the captain gestured towards Lia, "is Mr. Rupert Holmes. He is a journalist and novelist—if he ever finds the right muse, that is. The lovely lady to my right is Miss Honoria Porter, and her companion Miss Amelia Thompson is sitting next to Mr. Holmes."

"What a pleasure it is to meet all of you. I hope we have a pleasant two weeks at sea and become more than just acquaintances during this time," I said. My intention had been to sound polite and sincere even if I wasn't really sure I wanted to get to know anyone at this table better. I looked over at Mr. Holmes, who raised an eyebrow when our eyes met. Oh, I guessed what I said could be interpreted a few different ways. "That is, I hope that we all can become friends during this trip." I sat down, worried any attempt to not embarrass myself could cause more embarrassment.

"I know exactly what you mean, Miss Porter," Mrs. Wilcox chimed in. "It wasn't too long ago we were on a ship like this, headed to Brythion, looking for investors in my husband's emerald mines . . ."

Nelson Wright interrupted Mrs. Wilcox by clearing his throat.

"That is, my husband and Mr. Wright's emerald mines. They are in business together."

"I hope your trip was successful. If I had known you were there, I might have been able to arrange some meetings for you."

"It was quite successful. Thank you. We managed to get enough investors to continue mining for quite some time, as long as the mine continues to produce."

"You must have high-quality stones to convince those in the *ton* to invest."

"Of course, we used the necklace that my wife is wearing to demonstrate the quality of the stones. Why don't you show her, Violet?"

Violet nodded at her husband; it was clear that it had been a love match and not a business deal like so many marriages in Brythion. Violet reached up to unclasp the necklace around her neck. It was at that moment I saw it. There was no necklace.

Violet's eyes widened and her hands shook as she brought her hands down in front of her. "They are gone!"

"What did you say, Violet?" her husband asked, turning away from his food. He glanced down at her neck, confirming what Violet had just said.

"The jewels, they're gone."

*   *   *

Chapter Six

Somewhere on the Ocean, June 21, 1850

Dear Diary,

To say that today had been memorable would be an understatement. From actually boarding a ship headed to the New World, to sitting at a table with perfect strangers on the journey, to the missing necklace, and now this. I never would have imagined my journey would start like this.

*   *   *

Captain Castleberry took action immediately. He ordered the doors to the dining room closed, and all the rooms searched. If anyone was in their rooms, they were to be searched and then escorted to the dining room with the rest of us. I was impressed with how quickly he took charge of the entire situation, even if I didn't appreciate being held hostage in the dining room. It didn't matter that I understood why the captain had kept us all in the room. It had been a long day, and now some unknown person was pawing through my things. Things I didn't want others to know about, like the money I had and the stash of jewels I had sewn into the lining of my bags. I doubted anyone would find how I packed normal. So, now I was concerned that someone would steal what I had hidden, and I would have no way to prove any of it was mine, or I was going to be accused of stealing jewels and have no way to prove that I wasn't a jewel thief.

"Lia, they are going to find all the jewels I hid. I just know it," I whispered to my companion. "And while I didn't steal the jewels from anyone on this ship, are they really mine? Or were they merely on loan to me while I lived in my father's household? Have I been stealing from him this entire time?" I chewed on my lower lip, afraid I had been a thief since I was sixteen. It had never been my intention to steal from anyone, but maybe I had. And now I was using stolen funds to leave the country like a common criminal. And if I was a common criminal, why wasn't I a better one? How could I have been so shortsighted to book passage under my real name? What if my family sent someone after me, and by default, Lia? They would catch us and drag the two of us back in no time flat at this rate. I started pacing back and forth near the captain's table.

"Honoria, you have to calm down. If you keep going down this path, everyone is going to think you're guilty. Because you are acting guilty. The jewels sewn into your bags were given to you. They are yours. It makes sense that you took precautions to prevent them from being found. They are quite valuable. Really, everything makes perfect sense." Lia laid a hand on my shoulder, stopping me midstride. She turned me towards her, making sure I looked at her. "It's going to be okay. You've done nothing wrong."

"Nothing except run away from my family midseason with only a brief note left behind. And I used our real names when I booked passage. Whatever was I thinking? What if my parents sent someone after us?"

"Even if they do, it will take them a few days to catch up. By then we will be lost in a large city, and maybe even making our way to the next," Lia said, staring at me with her bright eyes. She held my gaze until I nodded in agreement with her.

Of course, that's when I saw a ship steward come into the dining room with my bags. I should say, with my empty bags. The steward glanced over at me briefly but strode directly over to the captain. This was exactly what I had been worried about. There was no way anyone was going to take me at my word. I was a young woman on my own, with no family to protect me. All they were going to see was a young lady who had hidden money and jewels in various places throughout her luggage.

The captain and steward looked in the bags and then looked up at me. Concern was written across the captain's face. Not what I was expecting. Maybe, just maybe, I had left a good enough impression on him that he wouldn't immediately jump to an unwarranted conclusion.

I touched the necklace I was wearing. This was an emerald necklace, and the Wilcoxes had said nothing about it. Did I even have another emerald necklace? Emeralds were my favorite stone, but they weren't easy to come by. Maybe I hadn't grabbed my other emerald necklace and the matching set of earrings, oh, and the bracelet. As those thoughts raced through my head, Captain Castleberry pulled out the emerald necklace I had just been thinking about. He looked up, caught me watching him, and raised an eyebrow. As efficient as he was starting the investigation, he also seemed rather nonchalant about everything.

I watched as he took the necklace over to the

Wilcoxes'. They both looked it over and shook their heads no. I could only assume they were letting the captain know it was not the missing necklace. I let out a sigh of relief. At least I wasn't going to be accused of being a jewel thief.

Captain Castleberry gingerly put everything back into my luggage. He grabbed the bags and strode over to me. "Miss Porter, they have finished searching your room. Might I suggest putting some of the valuables you are transporting into our ship's safe? I would not want you to have the same troubles as Mr. and Mrs. Wilcox."

"Thank you, Captain. I would very much like to take you up on your offer. I can meet you after you have finished with the investigation for tonight."

*   *   *

Chapter Seven

Somewhere on the Ocean, June 21, 1850

Dear Diary,

It would seem I did not completely understand what I was getting myself into when I set out on this journey. So far, very little has gone to plan, and now I'm on a ship, with only Lia to support me while I'm being accused of something I would never do.

*   *   *

"Did you see the emerald necklaces she has with her, plus the earrings and the bracelets? Who has that many emeralds? She has to be the person who stole my jewels. Nothing else makes any sense." Mrs. Wilcox's ample bosom jiggled as she stomped her foot, emphasizing her accusations. Her husband looked on bemused. I could not tell if he was distracted by his wife's cleavage or if he found her accusations amusing. Either way, he would not be any assistance in talking his wife out of her foolish accusations.

"Excuse me, are you accusing me of stealing your emeralds because I happen to have my own set of the jewels? Ma'am, that makes no sense at all. I have no reason to steal, as clearly I can afford to purchase my own jewels," I said, calmer than I felt. The last thing I wanted was to end up in a jail cell on a ship—tossed in the brig, that's what they called it.

"You have two emerald necklaces. How do I know you don't have more and one of them isn't mine?" Mrs. Wilcox jabbed my shoulder with her outstretched finger, punctuating her words.

"You are more than welcome to search my room again. You will see the only jewels I have with me are the one's I came with." I didn't feel like listening to any more accusations. I turned away, looking for the captain. Ah, there he was. "Come along, Lia, I don't plan on listening to this drivel any longer."

I turned on my heel, heading straight for our room. My emerald-green skirts swooshed around me. I stopped next to the captain.

"Mrs. Wilcox is trying to accuse me of stealing her jewels. Which is absolutely preposterous. If you could come by my room once you are done convincing her I didn't do it, I would love to keep my jewels in the safe while I'm on board. I cannot afford to lose any of them."

"Of course, Miss Porter. I will be around once I have calmed everyone down here."

I took one last look at the room. Mr. and Mrs. Wilcox were still by the captain's table. He was patting her shoulder like she was a prized hound as she cried over the missing gems. The man needed lessons on how to properly comfort a woman. Gwendolyn Wilcox sat at the table, clutching her handbag as if she was worried the thief was going to take it from her person. Nelson Wright was standing off by himself, an unlit cigar between his lips, hands in his pockets, looking more like a sullen teenager than a successful partner in an emerald mine. Then there was Mr. Holmes, also off on his own, standing near a door with his notepad out, taking notes on everything that was happening, or so I assumed. It made me wonder what he was actually writing down. I was going to have to figure out how to get my hands on that notebook.

Lia and I made it back to the room we were sharing. I let her through first, quickly shutting the door and leaning up against it.

"Can you believe this, Lia? We have to figure out what happened to those emeralds. I will not let them accuse me of stealing them. We need to find the real culprit."

"Why do you think they accused you?" Lia asked.

"I really don't know. I wonder if it has anything to do with the fact that we are two women traveling on our own without protection of any sort. At least they don't know of any. It does make me an easy target."

"That's ridiculous, miss–Miss Porter, you could never be an easy target."

"Thank you, Lia, and I don't intend on being one now. Which means we are going to have to find those jewels and whoever took them."

A powerful knock interrupted our discussion. "That must be the captain." I pinched my cheeks and bit my lips. "How do I look?"

"Lovely, miss–Honoria, you always look lovely." Lia was still struggling with being less formal, but she was trying.

I opened the door, and there stood Captain Castleberry. He was quite handsome. I bet he would be fun to spend some time with in an alcove.

"Let me just finish gathering everything." I walked

back to the dresser and collected my jewels. The captain stood in the doorway, patiently waiting for me to finish.

"Lia, I'm taking these jewels to the captain's safe. Knowing there's a jewel thief . . ." I shivered dramatically. I almost rolled my eyes at my theatrics, but I managed to keep a straight face. "It's so kind of you to offer your safe to protect my jewels, especially since so many people know what I have after that search."

"All part of the job, Miss Porter. I wouldn't want anyone on board to feel like they weren't safe. My crew and I will always be around to ensure no one has access to your jewels but you. If only Mrs. Wilcox had taken me up on my offer." Captain Castleberry offered me his arm, which I took as we walked down the corridor to his rooms.

"Poor Mrs. Wilcox. I can't imagine what she must be feeling having lost her jewels like that. I hope her husband isn't too angry with her."

"He shouldn't be. He's the one who refused the use of my safe. Said he felt better knowing they were with his belongings. Ironic that she was wearing the necklace when it went missing."

"Did you actually see it on her?"

"I did, before you made it down to dinner. I didn't notice it was missing until everyone else did."

"That's interesting." My mind whirled through the implications, putting together a suspect list in my head.

"Here we are." The captain opened the door to his cabin, letting me in first. He was quite the gentleman, leaving the door open behind us.

That was . . . somewhat disappointing. The captain was quite handsome and a flirt. He stepped around me, removing an ocean painting from the wall, revealing a safe. He turned the knob, stopping when he reached the coded number, then turning the opposite way. In moments, the safe was open. I stood on my tiptoes to put the jewels in, trying to see what was inside, but the safe was too high on the wall for me to look in. Until I felt two hands around my waist lifting me up suddenly. I dropped my bag of jewels in, noting a couple of other jewelry boxes, some gold coins, and a few different labeled stacks of banknotes. The captain set me down slowly. I turned towards him once my feet were on the floor. I grabbed the lapels of his jacket, pulled his head towards mine, and kissed him.

Before the captain could say anything, I slipped out of his grasp and out of his quarters.

*   *   *

Chapter Eight

Somewhere on the Ocean, June 21, 1850

Dear Diary,

You are going to think me quite scandalous, I just know it. I kissed the captain. He is handsome and his lips are appealing, so I did it. Then ran off like the silly girl I actually am. It's of no matter though, Lia and I have important business to attend to if I'm going to solve this crime for the Wilcoxes. I can't have them thinking I stole their jewels. It seems like a bad way to start in this new country.

*   *   *

I closed the door to my room behind me, leaning up against it to steady myself. My actions were shocking. I can't believe I had really gone and kissed the captain. I pressed my hand to my tingling lips. But there it was, proof I had lost my mind and done just that. I slowly slid to the floor, sitting with my back up against the door.

"Honoria, are you okay? Did something happen with the captain?" Lia asked, bending down in front of me, concern etched across her face.

"I'm fine. I might have lost my mind for a bit there, but nothing bad happened."

"I can't see you losing your mind. You're one of the most methodical people I know. If you weren't, we wouldn't be on this boat, in these fancy rooms, with funds to see us through. So what did you do that makes you think you've lost your mind?" Lia sat beside me on the floor, taking my hand in hers.

"I just kissed the captain."

"What?" Lia turned to look at me head-on. "Maybe you're right and you have lost your mind. What were you thinking?"

"His lips looked soft. I wanted to feel them on mine. That's what I was thinking, and I acted on those thoughts." I pushed myself up from the floor, not gracefully. My corset didn't allow for graceful. But I made it up to my feet. I brushed off my dress. "Come, Lia, we need to plan out this investigation. I do not want my name associated with jewel theft."

"You wouldn't want that, but if it's associated with kissing men you barely know, is that okay with you?"

"At least kissing is honest. Come to the table and sit. The captain said that Mrs. Wilcox was wearing the jewels when she sat down to dinner. Which rather limits the time they could have disappeared. It should limit the suspects as well, wouldn't you think?" I asked Lia, my mind going back to who was at the table and which of the crew served us.

"I don't rightly know, miss. I'm not a detective." Lia reverted back to calling me miss, I wondered if it was because she felt uncomfortable with the thought of investigating the missing jewels.

"You are now, Lia, you are now. Let's just pretend it's like the periodicals we've read together." I pinched the bridge of my nose, thinking through the tables in the dining hall. "It had to be someone at our table or a server. No one other than the crew approached during dinner."

"Since you're so cozy with the captain, you can ask him about the crew," Lia said.

Throwing my gloves at her, I teased her right back. "If I talk to the captain, you can handle Mr. Holmes. He seemed quite enamored with you at dinner."

"Is that so?" Lia smiled. "I would have never known by his conversation topic."

"Oh really? Why is that?" I asked.

"All he did was ask questions about you. The reporter seemed instantaneously lovestruck." Lia raised an eyebrow. She knew I didn't mind male attention, but I wasn't always the best at handling too much of it.

"Oh tosh! No one falls in love at first glance. That's not love, it's lust. Something they don't teach proper young ladies about. But they should."

"You should still use it to your advantage. I think you will have more success talking to him than I will. However, I should probably talk to Mrs. Wilcox. I'm not sure she realizes we are on this trip together, and she is unlikely to change her mind about you being the culprit until the jewels are back in her little hands."

"What do you mean she doesn't realize we are together? The captain clearly introduced you as my companion. She was sitting right there."

"I stepped out while you were . . ." Lia paused, "taking care of the jewels. I ran into Mrs. Wilcox. She proceeded to tell me all about her missing jewels, and how there was this redheaded flirt trying to trap the captain who must have stolen her jewels. I was so shocked I went along with it."

"What smart thinking! Yes, you speak to Mrs. Wilcox. We shall start tomorrow. I have a good feeling about this. Somehow this turn of events is going to help us on our journey."

*   *   *

Chapter Nine

Somewhere on the Ocean, June 22, 1850

Dear Diary,

I woke up with a smile on my face, and a solid plan in my head. I was going to clear my name of these foolish accusations. Really, who accuses someone of stealing emeralds simply because they had too many emeralds? It was quite a baffling theory, completely lacking in logic. But that's neither here nor there, the accusation was hanging over my head. I had a plan: talk to everyone at my table and figure out who the thief was—and maybe, just maybe, I would come across the captain and sneak in a few more kisses.

I was mostly thankful he had let me be last night. But the temptation of his lips was too much for me, and I want to feel them again. For scientific purposes, really. I need to ensure I get enough evidence on the feel of his lips to be accurate in my analysis.

*   *   *

I stretched in bed, languishing in the to-and-fro movement of the ship. It would be so easy to stay curled up under the blanket and let the rocking lull me back to sleep. Instead, I threw the covers off and pushed myself up into a sitting position. I had work to do if I was going to clear my name.

I looked over at the other bed. Lia was still fast asleep, her golden-brown curls cascading over the pillow. She looked so comfortable that I didn't want to wake her, even if it would have been much easier to get dressed if she was awake. I pulled my underthings out from my valise. Laying them on the bed, I contemplated the best way to tie myself into the multitude of layers. It wasn't until I got to the corset that I began to struggle, but with some wiggling and contortions, I was able to finesse my way into the contraption. After that, I grabbed an outfit that buttoned in the front, the sage green complimenting my hair and skin. It also brought out the color of my eyes. One look in the mirror confirmed it, I looked quite fetching.

Tiptoeing out of the room, I then shut the door behind me as quietly as possible. I let out a breath as I leaned against the door. I squared my shoulders and pushed myself off the door. I was on a mission to clear my name, and I was starting with Nelson Wright.

I made my way to the dining room with the thought that Mr. Wright was most likely at breakfast. However, after perambulating around the room and grabbing a croissant, I had not located my target. Exiting the dining room, I wandered to the bow of the boat. The morning sun glistened off the water. It was almost disconcerting to look out and not see land anywhere.

I shivered as the wind tugged at the hair falling loose from my hairpins. Glancing over to my left, I saw Nelson Wright. He looked to be contemplating life just as I was.

"Mr. Wright, what a pleasant surprise. Do you find the vastness of the ocean to be as awe inspiring as I do?" I brushed loose strands of my hair out of my eyes, trying to tuck them behind my ears.

"It is a lot of water," he said, barely glancing my way. Apparently, I was going to have to try much harder to get him to talk to me.

"That it is. Quite a bit of water. Do you live anywhere near the ocean?" I didn't really want to know where he lived. But it felt impertinent to just start asking him about his relationship with the Wilcox family.

"No. I live more inland, close to the mines. It's one of the reasons Mr. Wilcox and I are in business together," Mr. Wright said. It was nice that he had provided the perfect opportunity for me to discuss exactly what I wanted to discuss.

"How is working with Mr. Wilcox? He seems quite jovial."

"He is. He needs to take the business more seriously. He's lucky I wanted to invest in his project, even luckier that I'm willing to wed his daughter so he can keep the mines in the family."

"You're engaged to Gwendolyn?" I asked, unable to hide the shock in my voice.

"Yes. She is promised to me. We will be quite the couple in Nordu Anthropas, especially once she gets over her flights of fancy," Mr. Wright said, his face becoming unpleasantly pinched. I did not know Mr. Wright well, but he wasn't the type of man I would want to marry. If Gwendolyn was anything like me, she felt the same way. Mr. Wright saying his fiancée needed to get over "her flights of fancy," probably meant she needed to stop having independent thought.

"Why did you want to invest? You don't seem like the best match for Mr. Wilcox, or, I should say he does not seem to be the best match for you."

"You are quite right, Miss Porter. However, emeralds are quite lucrative and I hope to run the business before long. Mr. Wilcox has no sons, so it would only be natural for him to leave me the business as his son-in-law." Mr. Wright sniffed with disdain as he finished speaking. I couldn't tell if the disdain was for the Wilcox family or if it was because he wasn't running the business yet. Either way, Nelson Wright didn't like the family he was planning to marry into very much.

"And what about these stolen jewels? I hope you know I didn't take them. I have no need to steal emeralds, after all."

"They probably stole the necklace themselves and are filing an insurance claim for the loss. If I had thought about it, I would have done it."

With that last statement, Nelson Wright turned and walked away, leaving me there to ponder his word alone on the bow of the boat with nothing but the vast ocean before me.

Chapter Ten

Somewhere on the Ocean, June 22, 1850

Dear Diary,

I shouldn't be surprised at the machinations a daughter's parents will go through to find her a match. It seems even the most doting of parents lose the connection with their daughter once she is of marriageable age. Just look at what my mother had done. And now, to hear of poor Gwendolyn basically given to a man who refused to appreciate her . . .

*   *   *

Although it was difficult to leave the cool breeze and the sun behind, I didn't stay on the bow of the boat long. I turned to head back to the room Lia and I shared. I was in the hall outside our room when I heard someone crying. I stopped and listened, trying to determine where the sound came from. Walking past the door that led to Lia's and my room, I continued down the hallway. That's where I found Gwendolyn. She was indecorously plopped on the floor, her feet tucked under her pale-lavender skirts, and she was crying into her embroidered handkerchief.

"Oh dear Gwendolyn, whatever is the matter?" I asked.

"It's nothing," Gwendolyn sniffed. She looked at me, her eyes glossed over with water. Gwendolyn blinked a few times before her sobs shook her body.

"It's clearly not nothing." I sat down next to her on the floor, patting her leg in an attempt to comfort her. "There, there. Deep breaths, now. You can tell me whatever is bothering you."

"You'll think me silly. Most women would think I'm lucky to be in the position that I am in. But I don't feel lucky. I feel trapped," Gwendolyn said as she wept. I sat next to her, tucking my feet under my skirts, as her tears slowed to a trickle before continuing the conversation.

"You must be talking of your engagement to Mr. Wright, an unfortunate situation indeed," I said. I pulled a handkerchief out of my sleeve and handed it to Gwendolyn.

Gwendolyn looked up, shock stopping her tears completely. "How do you know about the engagement?"

"I was just speaking to Mr. Wright. He expressed some rather disturbing ideas about stopping your 'flights of fancy,'" I said.

"He *would* say something like that, just because I've offered my opinion on running the emerald mines." Gwendolyn sniffed.

"Mining gems must be so interesting. To take a rock from the earth and turn it into something someone wears. I've never even thought about what goes into it. What were your suggestions?" I asked, curious, to know more about this woman's interests and ideas.

"Revolutionary things that should not be revolutionary, like safety protocols for those working inside the mines, fair wages, limited hours, even potentially hiring women for the work that doesn't require going into the mine." Gwendolyn's face lit up as she spoke. She clearly cared about the people who allowed her to live the affluent lifestyle she was now living. Unfortunately, she was promised to a man who would never listen to her.

"Your ideas are extraordinary. I take it Mr. Wright doesn't agree with you?" It was all I could do not to roll my eyes at the thought of Mr. Wright agreeing with her. The man had mentioned committing fraud like it was nothing. My brief experience with the man made me feel like he didn't care for much of anything other than making money.

"Mr. Wright doesn't take the time to listen to me, so I'm not sure how he would even know if he agreed with me or not. The fact is, no one listens to me. Not Mr. Wright, and definitely not my parents, especially not my father."

"That's unfortunate. What have you tried to talk to your father about?"

"Mr. Wright—I cannot marry that man. I do not love him, he does not love me. I cannot see how either one of us will be happy together." Gwendolyn sighed as she twisted her embroidered handkerchief beyond recognition.

"You definitely should not have to marry such a man, or any man, for that matter. I know I plan on never marrying if I can help it," I said. The way Gwendolyn's eyes shot up to me as I said it indicated I spoke with excessive firmness. What could I say? It was ridiculous that women were still being married off with no say. This wasn't the Dark Ages. "I can help you come up with a plan to help you escape your dire circumstances. I don't want to see you stuck with

Nelson Wright any more than you do. The conversation I had with him was quite insufferable."

Gwendolyn nodded. "He is quite insufferable. You're correct, something needs to be done. I can't marry him."

"So, you'll let me help you?"

"I have a plan, Miss Porter. But, I'm quite concerned that there could be some unintended harm to those around me. I'm not sure how to limit the harm yet; I will figure it out though. I promise you I will. Thank you so much for talking to me. I feel somewhat less hopeless than I did a moment ago." Gwendolyn stood and walked away, only looking back to give me a wave and a smile.

For a moment, I sat there perplexed and a bit concerned. I wish Gwendolyn had shared her plan with me. Unintended harm was something I tried to avoid when making plans. Furthermore, I enjoyed a good plotting session, and it would have been quite amusing with a new acquaintance. Instead, I made my way back to my room. At least I could plot with Lia there. After all, there was a jewel heist to solve.

*   *   *

Chapter Eleven

Somewhere on the Ocean, June 22, 1850

Dear Diary,

I can't believe how willing men are to ignore the intelligence of women. Mr. Wright calling Gwendolyn's ideas "flights of fancy" sets my teeth on edge. It isn't right. I want to help Gwendolyn escape the life others have planned for her. I wonder if she would even want my help.

Sadly, I hadn't run into the captain during my excursions today. Which means I lack any new information where he is concerned. It is quite unfortunate.

*   *   *

The room was empty when I made it back. I was disappointed. I wanted to discuss with Lia what I learned about Nelson Wright and Gwendolyn Wilcox. Unfortunately, I was standing in an empty room. Time to reassess my next steps in this investigation. I needed to talk to Mr. and Mrs. Wilcox. I know Lia and I had agreed she would talk to them, but I wanted to see how they looked when they were questioned. Not that they would actually let me question them, since Violet Wilcox was sure I was the culprit.

Instead of trying to find the Wilcoxes like I so desperately wanted to, I took a moment to check myself in the mirror. Oh my, I couldn't leave the room with my hair in disarray. Taking a moment, I rebraided and pinned my hair into place as best as I could without Lia's assistance. I dabbed my eau de parfum behind my ears and left the room. I walked along the outside of the ship, the cool breeze refreshing after spending time in my stifling room. As I gazed over the railing, I took in the views of the ocean. It looked tranquil at the moment, but I had read how quickly things could turn from calm to tempestuous.

The clicking of footsteps behind me interrupted my reverie. I turned to see Nelson Wright looking around as if he was searching for someone. He had a velvet-covered box in his hand. I watched as Mr. Wright opened the door to the ship's corridor, peaking through it before stepping in. Interesting—it looked like he was sneaking around with a jewelry box. What I wouldn't give to search his rooms. I wondered if the captain would let me into Mr. Wright's room.

With that thought in my head (and not a single thought about kissing), I went in search of the captain. Along the way, I noticed Mr. Rupert Holmes in the corner, huddled over his notebook, writing furiously. Curiosity piqued, I made my way towards him. He was intense in his work, never acknowledging my presence.

"Ahem," I cleared my throat as I sat at the table where Mr. Holmes was working.

"I say, can you please—" Rupert Holmes looked up, noticing me for the first time. He started to stand, but changed his mind when he took in the fact I was already sitting. "I'm sorry, Miss Porter, my mind was occupied, and I did not see you arrive."

"Obviously, Mr. Holmes. What has you so occupied that you didn't even notice me?" I asked, leaning forward in the chair as I spoke.

"I'm trying to get my head around the jewel theft and who could be behind it. Clearly, you aren't involved in it.

The accusations made by Mrs. Wilcox are ridiculous as well as illogical."

"I can't help but agree with you. Have you learned anything interesting?" I tapped my fingers on the table. Like pacing, the repetitive motion helped me think.

"I feel like it has to be someone who was at our dinner table. But if it's not you or Miss Thompson, and it's not me, the only people left are the captain, Mr. Wright, and the Wilcoxes." Rupert Holmes tapped his pen against his teeth, falling back into thought, forgetting I was there, or so it seemed.

"And why should I believe you didn't steal the necklace? I can think of multiple scenarios where a fortune in jewels could help you out." I watched his reaction, which was indecipherable.

"Look at me." Mr. Holmes grabbed my hand and stared at me. It was so intense I moved to look away. "Really, look at me. Do you really think I stole the gems?"

He was looking at me so intensely that all I could do was shake my head no. His grey eyes reminded me of a stormy morning on the coast of Brythion. Our gaze stayed locked, and butterflies took residence in my midsection. It wasn't like I believed Mr. Holmes stole the jewels. I couldn't think of a probable reason, but that didn't mean he didn't have one, just that I didn't know what it was. I broke eye contact and looked down to where Holmes was still holding my hand. It was as if he forgot he had instigated physical contact. I looked back at him, unasked questions in my eyes.

"Miss Porter, I was able to talk to Mrs. Wilcox. You will never believe what she told me," Lia said as she rushed around the corner. "Oh, Miss Porter, I didn't realize you were with someone." Lia looked at me, then Mr. Holmes, and finally our entwined fingers.

Mr. Holmes released my hand as I withdrew it, catching Lia's eyes as I did so. Mr. Holmes shuffled through his notes, like he hadn't just been caught touching me.

"It's fine, Lia. I was just discussing the theft with Mr. Holmes. He's been attempting to figure out who stole the jewels as well." I gestured for Lia to sit.

"If that's the case, Mrs. Wilcox said some interesting things when we spoke. First, and probably the most interesting, is Mrs. Wilcox has other missing jewelry. She didn't realize the pieces were missing until after the emeralds went missing," Lia said.

"That is interesting, but it opens up the list of suspects to those not sitting at our table, including the staff on the ship. That will not make the investigation any easier." I felt my fingers tap on the table again. The plan Lia and I had put together last night needed to change. "Lia, why don't you see if you can talk to the staff, find out who has had access to the Wilcoxes' room?"

I stood, wiping my hands down the front of my dress. Sitting around was all well and good, but I was tired of planning and desperately needed to do something. Not to mention I was uncomfortable with the intense way Rupert Holmes looked at me. It was unlike anything I had ever experienced before. I wasn't sure if I liked it or not. That said, it excited me in ways I had never experienced before.

"It seems our time has come to an end for today. I hope you will expound on my reasons for stealing the jewels in the future, or at least give me an opportunity to gain your trust. Miss Porter, Miss Thompson, if you will excuse me."

Lia and I just watched as he gathered up his things and walked away.

*　　*　　*

Chapter Twelve

Somewhere on the Ocean, June 23, 1850

Dear Diary,

After the strange interaction with Mr. Holmes, I spent the rest of the day looking for either Mr. Wilcox or the captain. Somehow, I failed at finding either one of them. It wasn't until dinner that everyone was gathered again. And that was an awkward enough affair without me asking questions. Mrs. Wilcox spent the evening shooting daggers at me with her eyes. Apparently, logic would never fit into her explanation of where the jewels had gone. Rupert Holmes kept looking over at me in a way I can only describe as pensive. The captain tried to stay jovial and flirtatious, but the tension at our table made it difficult.

Adding to the tension at the dining table last night was the addition of Lucas Grantham. He was a last-minute passenger on the steamer ship. His obvious wealth left me with the impression he should have been at this table the night before but for some reason was left out. Mr. Grantham is the younger son of Earl Grantham and had been quite successful at amassing a fortune by investing in different businesses. He was one of the many investors Mr. Wilcox and Mr. Wright had entertained while in Fintan. Mr. Grantham was also quite smitten with Gwendolyn, or so it seemed. He could not take his eyes off her while we were at the dinner table. This development did not make Mr. Wright happy. I'm surprised he hadn't bored holes into the back of Mr. Grantham's head with the way he was glaring.

*   *   *

Lia had already left for the day; her goal was to talk to the staff that had access to the Wilcoxes' room. My goal for today was to succeed where I had failed yesterday. It was time to talk to Mr. Wilcox and, if I was lucky, the captain. I couldn't let his handsome face stop me from considering him as a suspect.

I decided to head to the back of the ship today. At last night's dinner, the captain mentioned that a small sitting area had been set up for us to enjoy the sun and the breeze as the journey continued. I walked along the outside of the ship, taking in the sun and salty air, not even concerned that the exposure was sure to add even more freckles to my face. The wooden planks creaked under my boots and the white-painted exterior of the ship reflected the bright day. As I stepped in front of an alcove, I heard a giggle. I glanced towards the sound and found Gwendolyn and Lucas together, laughing over something they both found quite amusing. Their flirtation was obvious to anyone who looked at them, the way she put her arm on his sleeve, how he brushed her hair off her cheek. It was clear Gwendolyn was enjoying the attention of Lucas Grantham. I filed that little bit of knowledge away as I continued to the back of the ship.

I turned the corner. The captain was there. I raised my hand to wave, but it appeared he was giving one of his staff a dressing down. I didn't want to interrupt or gain his attention, so instead, I snuck closer, hugging the wall as I attempted to remain unnoticed and hear his conversation.

"You were supposed to wait until we were closer to New Lankersham," the captain said to the young man he was talking to. I recognized him from my first day on the ship. I believed he was the crewman who escorted Lia and me to our room.

"I'm sorry, I didn't mean for it to happen, but there was no way around it," the young man answered, shuffling his feet as he did so.

"Miss Porter, how wonderful it is to see you," Mr. Wilcox said, his boisterous personality coming through in his greeting, at least in regards to the volume of his greeting.

It felt like I had jumped out of my skin. Fighting the urge to turn to where the captain and the crewman were, I ran my hands down the front of my dress, rolled my shoulders back, and took a deep breath before turning towards Mr. Wilcox. "How fortunate it is that you've found me. I came back here looking for you."

Mr. Wilcox turned an interesting shade of red while still puffing out his chest. Out of the corner of my eye, I saw the captain and his companion move away from the two of us. Clearly, they did not want to be overheard. I wondered if it was ship's business or something more nefarious. What if it was something criminal? All of my jewels were in his safe. Without those I might not have the means to continue this adventure I had started.

"Miss Porter, what has you out searching for me?" Mr. Wilcox asked, taking a seat as he did so.

"I was curious why you came all the way to Fintan to find investors? Didn't New Lankersham have enough interested parties for you to find individuals interested in your mines?" I sat across from Mr. Wilcox, leaning forward to illustrate my interest in whatever he had to say in response, putting aside my concerns for the future as I did so.

"There have been problems at the mines. The investors in New Lankersham are well aware of what's happening and refuse to invest until I sort everything out at the mines. I was trying to find investors who weren't so risk adverse, as they say." His shoulders slumped as he spoke.

"You mean, you were looking for investors who were less informed?" I heard the words fall from my mouth before I could stop them. I wanted to clamp my hand over my mouth to prevent myself from saying more. But it was already too late. I had put my foot in it for sure.

"Well, you see, that is to say—" Mr. Wilcox cleared his throat before continuing. "It's complicated. No need for you to worry your pretty little head about it."

Gwendolyn was right, her father too easily dismissed a woman's curiosity and intelligence. Which is why I continued on. "Really? I was actually curious about investing, but of course, I would need to know more. Like what sort of incidents have been occurring and what you plan to do about them. I spoke to Gwendolyn yesterday, and her ideas on the running and management of a mine are quite unique."

"Her ideas are interesting," Mr. Wilcox said with great care as if he was trying to determine what I thought about Gwendolyn's ideas.

"They are quite innovative. I could see where they would save your mines a lot of money in the long run, even though they require an influx of upfront capital right now." I was getting off-track, but if Mr. Wilcox wouldn't listen to Gwendolyn, maybe he would listen to me. I was still just a woman; however, I was also a very wealthy woman.

"That's one of the largest problems. After the last incident, I didn't have the money to invest. And the interested investors from Fintan only provided enough to cover damages from the incident." Mr. Wilcox wiped his forehead with his handkerchief. Despite the cool breeze, he was sweating rather profusely. "I will be able to do more once Mr. Wright hands over the capital to secure his partnership."

"Did you ever think of filing the insurance claim for the missing jewels?"

"If I had thought to insure them before the trip, I would do just that. But working with the families injured at the collapse and fixing all the damages caused by it occupied my mind. Insuring the necklace wasn't a top priority. Now I wish it was. The proceeds from the loss would have covered all the repairs and some additional safety measures. I'm happy I have enough to cover repairs, but this is too expensive to fix, so I want to do something to help prevent another incident in the future."

It seemed Mr. Wright was off-target when it came to his theory about who stole the jewels. However, based on what I'd just learned, Mr. Wilcox listens to his daughter more than she thinks. He at least cared about the people working for him more than it had originally sounded. Maybe I could help save her from her disastrous marriage and encourage her father to allow her to assist in running the business. After I clear my name, of course.

*   *   *

Chapter Thirteen

Somewhere on the Ocean, June 24, 1850

Dear Diary,

After overhearing the captain yesterday, I'm concerned that I trusted the wrong person with my jewels. If the captain is the thief, I'm in serious trouble. He has all of my jewels locked in his cabin. My current plan is to use those jewels to fund my trip if I have to. I know I have enough funds in my bank account, but I am worried some ill-informed banker would prevent my access.

I do feel like I'm making some progress on the case of the missing emeralds. I am suspicious of Nelson Wright, especially after the little slip from Mr. Wilcox about him not paying for his portion of the partnership. Then there is sweet Gwendolyn, who wants out of the situation her parents put her in. I know what it is like to be desperate. In fact, if I was in her shoes, I might take similar drastic steps. Finally, there is the captain. I don't know what his motive can be, but after that conversation . . . I just don't know if he is actually trustworthy.

On top of everything else running through my head, I keep circling back to the strange intensity that seems to vibrate between Mr. Holmes and me, I have never felt anything like it before. It is very different than the way I feel around the captain.

*   *   ***

Dinner had come and gone last night, and I still had not cornered the captain for a talk. I would not let another day go by without speaking to Captain Castleberry. To that end, I made my way to the bridge in search of the elusive man. The heels of my boots clicked on the wooden planks of the ship as I made my way to my destination for the day. Now and then, the ship would tilt, and my hand would reach out towards the white wall to steady myself. The wind tugged at my hair. Being on the sea had made my hair almost impossible to tame.

I climbed the stairs up to the bridge, grasping the railing as the ship suddenly tilted to the right. The sea was turbulent for the first time this trip. It was strange to feel like the ground was constantly being pulled from underneath me, and the constant movement was making my insides flip-flop. It was not the most pleasant feeling in the world.

"Miss Porter, what brings you to this part of the ship?" Captain Castleberry asked, his smile lighting up his eyes and showing off his dimples.

"I was hoping we could have a little chat. And, if you didn't mind, I wanted to grab a necklace out of your safe for dinner tonight." I glanced up at the captain, then down, smiling softly as I did so. The ship shifted at that moment, causing me to stumble directly into him.

He grabbed my elbow with one hand, while his other arm slid around my waist, ensuring I did not fall to the deck. "Whoa there, today is a good day to sit, rest, and enjoy the ride. It's not the best for being up and about, though. Let me escort you someplace where we can talk, and then we'll get your necklace."

I looked up at him, the thrill of being so close to him causing my insides to feel like butterflies had taken up residence there. It was slightly less unpleasant than the flip-flop the ship was causing. Mr. Holmes entered into my head unbidden, I shook my head, concentrating on the man in front of me, not the one invading my thoughts. "That would be lovely, Captain."

The captain offered his arm, which I took, and we made our way to the area where I had overheard the captain yesterday. "Mr. Grantham, how nice to see you. I hope you are enjoying the trip so far," the captain said.

"Captain Castleberry, have you been able to look into that matter we discussed earlier?" Mr. Grantham asked, barely glancing my way.

The captain looked at me out of the corner of his eye before responding. "I'm sorry for the confusion early on. I'm working on the other thing. Let's discuss it later, after I assist Miss Porter."

"Of course, I will come find you later today, when you aren't otherwise occupied," Mr. Grantham said. He gave a slight nod before leaving the area. I watched him walk away and saw out of the corner of my eye someone else leaving the area. Someone who didn't want to be seen.

"Miss Porter, what did you want to discuss?" the captain asked, tilting my head until our eyes connected. I didn't want to believe he was the thief. Yesterday's conversation was weighing on my mind. I needed to know what it was about. And now there was this strange interaction with Mr. Grantham that only raised more concerns. The question was, should I be subtle or just come out and ask the captain? I raised an eyebrow before looking away.

"Can I be blunt, Captain?"

"Of course, it seems that's more your nature."

"Yesterday you were scolding your crewman for doing something too early. It was supposed to happen closer to shore. What were you talking about?" I looked the captain in the eye, trying to analyze his reaction.

He laughed—not the reaction I was expecting at all. "Do you think I took the necklace? That I'm running an international jewel theft crew while captaining a ship?"

"Do I want to think you are an international jewel thief? No, I don't. But you have to admit it is a possibility. And you didn't actually answer my question." I looked at him with a sly smile.

"Of course, Miss Porter, I do apologize. It has to do with a matter Mr. Grantham and I are working on. I wish I could tell you more." The captain gathered my hands into his, his eyes asking me to believe him. "I can take you to the safe and show you that your jewels are secure. I assume that's why you want to grab a necklace."

"That would be lovely. I appreciate your understanding." I stood on my tiptoes and kissed his cheek, right where his dimple showed itself when he smiled.

*　　　*　　　*

Chapter Fourteen

Somewhere on the Ocean, June 25, 1850

Dear Diary,

Another day come and gone, and I still don't know who stole the necklace. Although, I do have my suspicions. And now I want to know what's going on with the captain and Lucas Grantham. Even though my jewels were still sitting in the captain's safe, I'm not convinced of the captain's lack of involvement.

*   *   *

I needed to talk to Gwendolyn again. I was certain she had taken her mother's necklace to save herself from marriage to Nelson Wright. But I had no proof. None of us saw her take it at the table. In fact, I don't even remember Mrs. Wilcox wearing a necklace. The theft must have occurred before Lia and I arrived at the dinner table. It was the only explanation.

I left Lia sleeping in bed once again. Lia's love for sleeping in gave me the time to improve my skills at fixing my hair. I was getting better at taming my unruly hair. Was it stylish? No. But the chignon at the base of my neck did the trick and kept me looking proper. It hid my true nature as a wild child.

The ship shifted as I made my way to the bow. I stumbled and grabbed onto the metal railing to steady myself. Moments like this increased my ever-present concern of falling overboard. A concern I spent most of the day ignoring.

The wind whipped across the bow of the boat, pushing me away from the railing I clung to. I questioned the wisdom of walking around anywhere outside while the weather was this volatile. As if the ocean agreed with me, the ship lurched, and a wave crashed against the hull, drenching my dress and the railing I clung to. My fingers, frozen from the wind and the water, slipped from the railing, I stumbled backward. My heart leapt from my chest as the ship tilted the other way. I was going to fall overboard. I just knew it.

That's when I felt an arm slip around my waist, pulling me back into the hard body of a man, away from the cold and turbulent ocean. Turning to thank the rescuer, I found myself staring up into the eyes of Rupert Holmes. In that moment, my breath left my body, and I felt like I had no way to get it back again. So, I stood there in his arms, gasping for breath, grasping for some words, any words to say.

"Miss Porter, are you okay?" Mr. Holmes asked as he looked down at me. I just stared back at him, still unable to say anything, until he raised an eyebrow.

"Thank you, Mr. Holmes. I was afraid I was headed into the great deep. Oh my, I'm getting you all wet. I'm so sorry." I tried to take a step back, but the ship lurched again, sending me careening back into Rupert—um, I mean Mr. Holmes.

I felt his other hand at my waist, steadying me. "Do not concern yourself with that. I'm glad you are okay. We wouldn't want you swimming with the fishes now, would we?"

"No, Mr. Holmes, we would not." I looked from his eyes to his mouth and bit my lip. Stopping my errant thoughts, I looked away. "Would you be ever so kind and escort me back to my room? I'm afraid I must change out of this ensemble before I catch my death of a cold. But I would love to have a chat indoors, where it is safe and we can sit." I felt water drip down my forehead and my wet hair stuck to my cheek. "I just need a moment to put myself to rights."

"Of course, Miss Porter, you have me intrigued. Whatever could you want to talk to me about?" Mr. Holmes shifted me so I was beside him, putting himself between me and the sea, his arm was still wrapped around my waist. He opened the door to the interior of the ship, allowing me to step through first.

I walked with him in silence, not moving away from his light embrace until we stood in front of the door to my room. As we stopped, he took my hand. I could feel his warmth through my damp glove. "I will wait for you at the table we sat at before." He raised my hand to his lips and kissed it, his eyes, never breaking contact with mine, then walked away. I stood there, stunned.

*   *   *

Having changed into a warm green wool dress, I made my way back to the table where I knew I would find Mr. Holmes. And he was there, bent over papers, his brown bowler resting on the table. I slipped into the chair across from him, grabbing one of his papers to look at. It had Gwendolyn written on it with a question mark next to it. His thoughts appeared to align with mine regarding the jewel theft. I set the paper back onto the table.

"Mr. Holmes, I was curious if Gwendolyn left the table before Lia and I arrived the night the necklace was stolen? I don't think Violet Wilcox had her emeralds on when we sat down to dinner. But we were late."

"Let me think . . . The captain escorted us all to our seats. He mentioned that there would be two more joining. The first course was served. Mr. Wright said something repugnant." Mr. Holmes paused. It was like I could see his thoughts running through his head as he replayed the events of the first dinner. He looked up at me. "She did, right after the first course was served. She kissed her mom on the cheek and left. She wasn't gone for long, but it was long enough to stash the necklace somewhere. She had just sat back down when you arrived."

"That must have been when she took them. It had to be her. I'm assuming she did it to get away from Nelson Wright. Who could fault her for wanting to marry him? He calls her ideas frivolous, even though they would save lives." I looked up and saw the captain and Mr. Grantham talking. They were almost out of sight, like they were trying not to be noticed. Glancing around the room, I noticed Nelson Wright watching the captain and Mr. Grantham. I swear I saw hatred in his eyes, and I couldn't figure out why.

"I need to find Gwendolyn. I don't want her to be stuck with Mr. Wright. There has to be some way to clear my name without implicating her." I stood.

"That's rather noble of you, trying to help her out, even though she is willing to let you take the fall for her crime," Mr. Holmes said under his breath as he stood.

"Maybe, but being trapped in marriage is a fate I wouldn't wish upon any woman, so I need to help her."

I looked around the room before I left. The captain, Mr. Grantham, and Mr. Wright were gone. I walked to Gwendolyn's room. Before I got there, I had the unfortunate pleasure of running into Mr. Wright, quite literally.

"Oh, Miss Porter. You should watch where you're going. I didn't see you coming around the corner," he explained in clipped tones but did not apologize.

"Where are you off to in such a hurry, Mr. Wright?"

"I need to finish some discussions with Mr. Wilcox about the mines. I doubt it would be of any interest to you. Business rarely interests a lady."

"Are you going to pay Mr. Wilcox for your part of the partnership? I've heard it would make a tremendous difference to the working conditions of the miners," I said, not moving out of his way. With all my petticoats on, Nelson Wright would have to step around me to go downstairs. Since he had irritated me with his comments, my miniature rebellion was not without cause.

"What is it with women and their talk of working conditions?" Mr. Wright said as he pushed by me.

*   *   *

Chapter Fifteen

Somewhere on the Ocean, June 26, 1850

Dear Diary,

I can't believe I almost went overboard yesterday. Maybe I'm being dramatic, but there was a moment when I thought my life was over. And then Mr. Holmes wrapped his arms around me, saving my life.

There is something happening between Mr. Holmes and me. It leaves me short of breath and extremely confused. I may even be more confused about my reaction to Mr. Holmes than I am about the jewels. At least I have theories about the jewels. I don't like all my theories, but I do have some.

*   *   *

"Lia, that man is insufferable. I can't believe he's managed to convince Mr. Wilcox he's good for the mines and for Gwendolyn." I shut the door behind me and began pacing our tiny room. "He's not good for anyone or anything."

"I take it you've had another run in with Mr. Wright, or should I say Mr. Wrong." Lia giggled, laughing at her own little play on words. It was nice to see Lia come out of her shell. Every day, she acted more like a friend and less like a servant.

"I did. I asked him about the money he owes Mr. Wilcox and he blew me off, pushed right on by me. There's just something about him. I can't put my finger on what it is exactly . . ." Lost in thought, I stopped pacing.

"Are you sure it's not just that he has no compassion for others and dismisses everything anyone says, unless he's the one speaking?" Lia asked as she pinned her hair into place.

"Oh, what did you just say? I'm afraid my mind trailed off for a bit."

"What's weighing on you, Miss . . . Honoria?" Lia asked. She focused all her attention on me.

"I don't know. No, that's not true, I do know. I think Gwendolyn took her mother's necklace to escape a marriage she doesn't want. How can I get her in trouble for something that I did myself? She deserves a happy life." I sighed, sitting down on my bed.

"Are you sure Gwendolyn has the jewels? You've mentioned seeing several others sneaking around the ship. There's the captain, Mr. Grantham, and even Mr. Wright. Maybe it's not as simple as just Gwendolyn taking the necklace; it seems everyone has secrets."

"You aren't wrong, Lia. It seems almost everyone on this vessel is hiding something from someone. I guess it's time I try to find out what those secrets are. It could only help."

"It couldn't hurt. In fact, I overheard something just this morning." Lia leaned forward in her chair.

"Oh really, whatever did you 'overhear?'" I asked. Lia definitely meant she was eavesdropping when she said she overheard. But I could let that slide, for the most part.

"I was looking for one of the crew to talk to; I wanted to see if I could get more information on Mr. Grantham. He's been such an enigma, and it's driving me crazy. Instead of finding them, I came across the captain and Mr. Grantham talking. I did my best to stay out of sight, but I also didn't want it to look like I was hiding. Thankfully, one skill I have developed as a servant is to be inconspicuous. I grabbed myself a cup of tea and sat at a nearby table." The smirk on Lia's face said it all. She was rather proud of her spying ability.

"That was smart, creating a reason for you to be there. Now what did they talk about? Was it the jewels?" I asked, trying to keep the impatience out of my voice.

"It wasn't the jewels, at least I don't think so. They were discussing someone on board that's a con artist. Mr. Grantham almost invested in someone's business. That's how Mr. Grantham amassed his fortune: shrewd investments. But after a bit of research, he discovered the person was a fraud, a con artist. And the person is on the ship. Can you believe it?"

"Really? That's interesting. Did they ever mention a name?"

"No, they didn't. I would have stayed longer, but the captain saw me there, so I finished my tea and left. I tried to be as normal as possible," Lia said, she sounded disappointed that she didn't get more information.

"I wonder who they could have been talking about? And if it has anything to do with the missing emeralds."

"Apparently Mr. Grantham wanted to stay unknown on the ship. But someone on the crew introduced him to Mr. Wright and Gwendolyn, ruining whatever he had planned. The captain wasn't very happy about it. I think it has something to do with trying to catch the con artist."

"Lia, you got so much information today. I'm impressed."

Lia blushed and looked away for a moment. "Do you think the con artist is someone at our table? There's not many people it could be."

"True, it is a very limited suspect pool. Maybe it's the con artist that took the necklace," I said. "It would be nice to find out that Gwendolyn didn't take them." I really wanted to help Gwendolyn escape her fate, which was harder to do if I was believed to be the thief. Granted, I was pretty sure only Violet Wilcox thought I stole her emeralds.

"You should talk to Gwendolyn. You could tell her about your escape. I bet she would open up to you even more," Lia said.

"It's like you're a mind reader. I really want to talk to her, but I haven't been able to find her anywhere on the ship."

"I see her inside more often than outside." Lia offered.

"That's understandable," I responded. The sensation of flying toward the railing ran through my body, sending chills up my spine.

*   *   *

Chapter Sixteen

Somewhere on the Ocean, June 27, 1850

Dear Diary,

I am positive that Gwendolyn is avoiding me. It should not be this hard to have a conversation with someone while on board a ship. There's nowhere for them to run off to. And yet, I still have not sat down with Gwendolyn. I had planned to corner her after dinner last night, but somehow, she slipped away without me even noticing. Okay, fine, I might have got a little carried away flirting with the captain. He's so easy to be around and too much fun to flirt with. I think it's because I know it will not lead anywhere. There's no pressure or expectations. Just a bit of fun banter to stay entertained. I wish any of my seasons had been like this. But there was always the pressure to marry, so being seen with any man, especially seen flirting with them, was like declaring your interest in a forever. How does one even know if an interest would last forever? Especially when you aren't ever allowed to see who a person really is.

That's why I enjoy flirting with the captain. I don't really care who he really is, as long as he isn't the thief. And really, after what Lia overheard, he seems more interested in catching criminals than being one. All I really care about right now is having a bit of fun and finding out who really has those emeralds.

*   *   *

"I swear, Lia, I don't know how she does it. Gwendolyn is like a ghost when she wants to be. I know she's around, but I can't seem to find her. Do you know how many times I've walked up and down these halls?" I gesticulated as I spoke, my hands and arms flailing here and there. I sighed; I was getting so tired.

"Have you tried any of the more secluded spots, Honoria?" Lia stood, looking her most prim and proper.

"What do you mean?" I stopped pacing to look at Lia.

"I just noticed her making eyes at Mr. Grantham last night at dinner. And he responded with interest. Plus, I've seen them around the boat every now and then. I believe they are quite interested in each other," Lia said. "Aren't you an expert on alcoves?"

"Hilarious, Lia." I laughed. "But I do see what you are saying."

I made my way to the area of the ship where I saw Gwendolyn and Mr. Grantham together. I couldn't believe Lia was right. There they were, almost hidden in the same alcove I saw them in last time.

"Gwendolyn, Mr. Grantham, how lovely it is to see you here, together. What a surprise." I said.

Gwendolyn jumped away from Mr. Grantham as if a fire had erupted between them. "Miss Porter, how . . . I mean . . . um . . ."

"Miss Porter, how nice it is to see you again outside of the formal dinner," Mr. Grantham said, bowing slightly as he did so.

"Yes, it is lovely. I was wondering if I could steal Gwendolyn away for a moment? I have something of the utmost importance I would like to discuss with her."

Mr. Grantham looked over at Gwendolyn, a question clear in his eyes. Gwendolyn gave a slight nod in the affirmative. I breathed a sigh of relief, happy she had decided to talk to me.

"I will talk to you later, Miss Wilcox." Mr. Grantham kissed her hand and left the two of us to talk.

"Thank you so much for talking to me. I have a feeling you've been avoiding me, and I think I know why," I said, sitting down beside Gwendolyn.

"I haven't . . . that is. Oh, Miss Porter, I think I made a mistake, and now I've messed up everything." Tears ran down Gwendolyn's cheek.

"It's okay, Gwendolyn, we will fix it. Everything is going to be fine." I patted her hands, trying to console her.

"It will never be fine. I'm going to be stuck married to Mr. Wright for the rest of my life. There's no way for me to escape it now." Gwendolyn's voice cracked as she sobbed.

"Don't you have the emeralds? Isn't that your plan to escape the marriage?" I asked.

She looked up at me, her face red and splotchy. "How do you know that?"

"I escaped my own unwanted marriage. I took all the jewelry my father had given to me. It's one of the ways I'm paying for this trip."

"You ran away from marriage? That's what I want to do. I was planning on using the necklace to fund my escape," Gwendolyn said, shocked, her eyes drying up as we continued to speak.

"Let's go to your room. Grab the necklace. We can put it back in your mother's jewelry box." I stood up, waiting for her to follow me.

"Okay, we need to put together a story." Gwendolyn said pensively.

"That shouldn't be hard. In fact, it will be the easy part," I said.

"Here we are. Let me just unlock the door." Gwendolyn turned the key and pushed open the door. "I've kept the necklace with my other jewels. I thought it would be inconspicuous there if anyone searched."

"That makes perfect sense." I watched as Gwendolyn opened her jewelry box. She stared at the box for a moment, and then she grabbed one piece of jewelry after another, almost throwing each one onto the table. Finally, she flipped the jewelry box upside down, shaking it. Nothing came out.

She looked up at me, tears glistening in her eyes. "They're gone. My mother's emeralds are gone."

"Gone? What do you mean, gone?" I asked, confusion laced through the words.

"Someone took the necklace I stole. How could something like this happen? How many people knew I had the emeralds?"

"I don't know, Gwendolyn. But I think I know who has the necklace now. We just need a plan to catch the culprit with the necklace." I drummed my fingers on the table as a plan started to come together.

*   *   *

Chapter Seventeen

Somewhere on the Ocean, June 28, 1850

Dear Diary,

I'm shocked that Gwendolyn no longer has the emeralds. My plan had been to sneak them back into Violet Wilcox's jewelry box and try to convince her that she only thought she had put them on that night, but in the excitement of the journey, had forgotten to actually wear the necklace. So much for that plan. The emeralds are still missing. While I think I know who has them, I don't think the person would want to give them back, at least not as easily as Gwendolyn had been to convince.

The difference was Gwendolyn was acting out of desperation, whereas the second thief was in it for the money. Or at least that's what I assumed.

*   *   *

"Captain, I was hoping I could talk to you for a moment?" I called out as I saw him cross the stern of the ship. He looked handsome in his uniform, but that was not important right now, even if he was hard to ignore.

"Of course, Miss Porter. How can I help you?" He stopped midstride, waiting for me to catch up.

"I wanted to talk to you about the missing emeralds and what you have been discussing with Mr. Grantham. I believe they are related. Although, I don't know much about what you are plotting. Just the little bit Gwendolyn learned from Mr. Grantham," I said, explaining the little I knew as we walked. To be honest, it wasn't much.

"You are lacking in details, aren't you, Miss Porter?" He smiled at me.

"You see my dilemma, Captain. I have a vague idea of what is going on, but I'm lacking a considerable number of details." I gave him a coy smile in return, looking up at him through my eyelashes. It was my goal to convince him to help, and if it took some mild flirting to get my way, well… I wasn't opposed to employing such tactics.

"You are a persistent woman, aren't you? I'm surprised you're still looking for the emeralds. I assumed you would give up after a day or two." He ran his hand through his hair. The captain didn't look pleased with my perseverance.

"It illustrates how little you know about me. Which isn't surprising: we have only known each other for a few days. You should know that this is no longer just about the emeralds. It's about a young lady's happiness. I can't turn my back on her, in fact, I refuse to. Gwendolyn and I have more in common than you would think. So, will you help me by filling in some of the details I'm missing?" I fluttered my lashes as I glanced up at the captain.

"It wouldn't be very polite of me if I didn't share now that I know a young lady's happiness is at stake." Captain Castleberry stopped at a table. "Please, have a sit. This could take a while."

My deep green skirts flared out as I sat. I leaned forward, anxious to hear what the captain would say next.

"It seems you've heard that there is a con man onboard my ship. Mr. Grantham is a keen investor." The captain held up his hands, anticipating my interruption. "It's easier to start early on. It will all make sense by the time I'm done. Where was I? Oh yes, Mr. Grantham is a keen investor. About a year ago, a man approached him regarding a potential investment in hot-air balloon travel. Mr. Grantham was incredibly interested, until he did some research. There was no company, no hot-air balloons, no pilots, nothing." The captain leaned back in his chair.

"Oh dear, it was a fake business. There was nothing there at all." I was amazed at the lengths this man had gone just to take people's money.

"Worse, the man had taken money from most of the aristocracy living in Fintan at the time. Mr. Grantham barely escaped. There was so much pressure to invest, and invest in a hurry." The captain tapped the table with his index finger. "It became interesting when this man showed up in Fintan again, now talking about emerald mines in Eletharis."

My eyes widened. "It can't be Mr. Wilcox. Can it?" I plucked at the trim of my skirt, worried for Gwendolyn.

"The Wilcoxes have emerald mines. Some really promising mines. From everything I've heard, they should produce for years and years. Especially if they are managed properly."

"That's a relief. I'm happy to hear Mr. Wilcox is an honest man. I would hate for Gwendolyn to discover everything she knows is false." My mind was racing connecting the dots and creating a plan to expose the culprit.

This information narrowed down the suspects to a very fine point. Unfortunately, figuring out how to catch the thief was not coming together as quickly as I would like.

"Do you think he has the emeralds?" the captain asked looking towards me. It seemed both the captain and I had latched on to the same culprit after eliminating Mr. Wilcox.

"I do. It's imperative that I get into his room. The room needs to be searched for the necklace before he suspects we are on to him. The emeralds must be found, not only to clear my name, but also to help Gwendolyn." I looked at the captain. Our eyes locked. "Please, can you help?"

"How can I say no to your gorgeous green eyes?" He leaned in towards me.

"I don't think you can say no." I leaned a little closer to him.

"Since that's the case, I could misplace my keys. I do have access to every room." He pulled the keys out of his pocket and set them on the table.

I snatched the keys and stood up. "Thank you. I'll be sure to get these back to you as soon as I can."

Slipping the keys into my pocket, I left the captain sitting there, looking bewildered. I rushed down the hall to my room. Lia needed to be part of the next phase of my plan.

"Lia!" I called out as I entered our room.

"I was just about to leave, Honoria. I'm in desperate need of some fresh air," Lia said, grabbing her coat and scarf. It was always cold out on the bow.

"Let's go." I held the door open for Lia. "I have keys to all the rooms. His room needs to be searched soon."

I continued to outline the rest of my plan as we walked along the bow of the boat. If it all went well, everyone but the culprit would get what they wanted. Gwendolyn could marry who she wanted. Her father would have a real investor, and my name would be cleared.

*   *   *

Chapter Eighteen

Somewhere on the Ocean, June 29, 1850

Dear Diary,

Everything is in place to catch a thief. Lia has been indispensable to this plan. I don't know what I would have done without her. I'm so happy she's along on this journey with me. Especially pleased that she is enjoying herself as well. I'm starting to feel that I truly have a friend and companion with me, rather than a servant. Especially now that I fix my hair each morning instead of waking her up.

Back to catching a thief: I have all my ducks in a row. It's time to start knocking them down.

*   *   *

Lia and I made our way down to the dining room. The two of us had spent the last day and a half making sure everything was in place to unmask the thief tonight— figuratively speaking, of course. Yesterday, Lia searched the culprit's room. She found the velvet box with the necklace in it, proving what I already suspected.

Instead of chasing down our culprit, the plan was to catch him during dinner time. He would then be held away from the other passengers until we docked, and he could be handed over to the authorities. The captain had sent a telegraph ahead so the local police should be waiting for the thief.

The waiting had my nerves on end. I knew everything was in place. Lia had taken the velvet box with the necklace. The plan was to slip it into his frock coat pocket before discussing the theft at the table. During the discussions, I was certain the thief would interrupt, providing an opportunity to search pockets and find the necklace. That's at least how the evening was supposed to go. I was concerned that all the planning would go off the rails.

I passed the day away outdoors trying to read. It was a lovely time to be outside. After I almost went overboard because of the sea's turbulent waves, I was much pickier about when I spent time outside. The ocean needed to be peaceful; the wind needed to be a gentle breeze, not the terror it had been the other day.

"Miss Porter, taking a break from finding the thief?" Mr. Holmes asked, interrupting my reading.

"Do you think I would take a break if I hadn't figured it out already?" I raised an eyebrow at Mr. Holmes.

"I do not. I assume that means you solved it." Mr. Holmes sat down, taking off his bowler hat and resting it on his knee. "Are you going to share?"

"No, I'm not going to share. You're going to have to wait like everyone else." I stood, squeezing his shoulder before walking away.

* * *

The hours before dinner had finally passed. I was dressed in my finest green silk gown with an off-the-shoulder bodice that set off my favorite emerald necklace perfectly. I swept my hair back into a chignon with emerald pins to give a bit of sparkle to my red hair. Before I went to dinner, I bit my lips and pinched my cheeks to give them a bit of color. Lia followed me wearing my blue velvet gown. It had taken days to convince her to borrow some of my clothing for these dinners. The blue looked stunning on her. In fact, I should probably just let her have the gown. It looked better on her than it did on me. And she needed some fancier clothes as my companion.

We entered the dining room, just like we did every other night. Tension was different for the two of us, though; tonight was different. Tonight, we would catch a thief. I nodded to Lia as I took my seat next to the captain. She made her way around the table, walking behind the Wilcoxes and Mr. Wright. Gwendolyn pushed back her chair suddenly, causing Lia to trip.

"I'm so sorry, Miss Wilcox, I can't believe how clumsy I am," Lia said, pressing her hands to her bodice as if she was trying to shrink.

"It's my fault. I should have watched what I was doing," Gwendolyn said, pulling her chair back into place at the table. Lia made her way to her seat next to Mr. Holmes.

"Are you trying to rub in the fact that my emeralds are still missing by wearing so many of them, Miss Porter?" Mrs. Wilcox fanned herself with one hand, clasping her husband's hand with the other.

"No, Mrs. Wilcox, I just like emeralds. My father always gave them to me, saying they sparkled just like my eyes," I said.

"Your father was correct." The captain smiled as he spoke. "Why don't we eat?" He nodded to the staff, letting them know to serve.

"I've actually been working on building a case against a con man on this trip. The man conned men out of their money by asking for investments in fake business," the captain added, his eye on me.

"I wonder if he also stole the emeralds?" I mused.

"Wait, a con man?" Mr. Wilcox asked, his mustache twitching. "What type of business did this man ask people to invest in?"

All eyes turned to Mr. Wilcox when he joined the conversation.

"Why are we even talking about this? A con man. It can't have anything to do with us or the emeralds." Mr. Wright waved his hand as if he was dismissing the conversation.

"But I think it does. I think whoever the captain is after stole the emeralds as a last-ditch effort once he knew he was in trouble," I said, leaning forward over the table.

Mr. Wright stood, his chair tipping until it fell on the floor. The noise caused everyone in the dining room to look at us. A servant scurried over, righting the chair.

"Sit down, Mr. Wright. You are causing a scene for no reason," Mrs. Wilcox said.

"No reason? Don't you see she is accusing me of the theft?" Mr. Wright's face was an unusual shade of red. I was afraid he was going to have an aneurysm or fit of some kind.

"Why do you think Miss Porter is accusing you of anything?" Mr. Holmes asked. "She's said nothing of the sort. In fact, it seems like she's just sharing ship gossip."

"Are you all just willfully ignoring what she is implying?" Mr. Wright said, spittle spraying as he spoke.

"We can end this right now if you want, Mr. Wright. You could prove your innocence. Just empty your pockets," I said with a shrug.

"Fine, I'll empty my pockets, and we can end this conversation, discuss something more pleasant." Mr. Wright reached into the pockets of his frock coat and stopped. "We should all just go back to eating dinner." Mr. Wright bent to sit down.

The captain stopped him. "Empty your pockets, Mr. Wright, or I'll do it for you."

Mr. Wright stood there, hatred in his eyes. He pulled his hand out of his pocket. In it was a sparkling necklace.

"My emeralds. You took them!" Mrs. Wilcox said.

"He did, in fact, take them. Mr. Wright is the con man the captain has been looking for," Mr. Grantham said. "He tried to get me to invest in his hot-air balloon company. Luckily, I found out it was fake before I handed over my money."

"Is that why you've yet to hand over your investment in the mines? You never planned on paying, did you?" Mr. Wilcox asked, his face turned red as he glared at Mr. Wright.

Once again, the captain nodded, this time letting the crew know it was time to take Mr. Wright into custody.

*   *   *

Chapter Nineteen

Somewhere on the Ocean, June 30, 1850

Dear Diary,

What a relief to have finally figured out who had the emeralds! I never would have expected it to be so complicated. Can you imagine someone stealing something that you stole? I can hardly believe that's what happened, even though I'm the one who figured it out. Even better than solving the crime of the missing emeralds was freeing Gwendolyn from an awful marriage. Mr. Wright is the worst sort. Not only is he a criminal, but he is also completely misogynistic. I find the second character trait to be the worse among the two.

I still feel like I have one more thing to take care of before the end of this part of my journey. I hope it goes well and my meddling doesn't offend.

*   *   *

After Mr. Wright was arrested last night, the Wilcoxes retired for the evening. I had hoped to speak with them, but Violet Wilcox was overcome with emotions and needed a place to calm her nerves, or so she said. I believed her continued accusations embarrassed her, and she was trying to recover. However, I had no intentions of holding that against her.

Instead, after a decent night's sleep, I decided to take a turn around the ship, hoping to run into my fellow passengers, most specifically Mr. Wilcox. I made my way to the lovely sitting area towards the back of the ship. That area is where I most often saw the gentlemen together; granted, they were normally discussing some scheme or another. It was my hope that this time I could propose a course of action they deemed worth following.

"Miss Porter, just the person I wanted to see." Mr. Wilcox waved at me as I stepped into the sitting area. "Come, come, have a seat. We have much to discuss, you and I."

"Mr. Wilcox, I was looking for you. I was hoping to talk to you about . . .," I said.

"Sit. Let's talk. First, I cannot thank you enough for finding my wife's emeralds and unmasking Mr. Wright. To think I trusted him enough to go into business with him and let him propose to my daughter. I was such a fool." He wiped his forehead, removing the sweat beading there. I knew I probably should have told him he wasn't a fool, but I wasn't here to soothe injured pride.

I sat, smoothing my blue plaid skirts as I did so. "Actually, Mr. Wilcox, I wanted to talk to you about Gwendolyn."

"You do?"

"Yes, I believe she feels overlooked when it comes to the business of the mines, and she has a lot of great ideas. Instead of trying to find a man to partner with you, why don't you teach your daughter how to run the mines? I believe she would be very much interested in doing so."

"She has made suggestions, and I do intend to follow them in the future. But I can't leave her the mines. If she were to marry, she would lose everything. I can't guarantee her future that way. Not to mention, I need an influx of cash, an investor or partner, to fix the safety problems that currently exist."

"I think you'll find the solution to that on this ship as well." I smiled.

"Who? Are you suggesting yourself, Miss Porter?" Mr. Wilcox asked.

"Unfortunately, I cannot invest at the moment. But I wish I could. I was actually speaking of Mr. Grantham. I believe he is interested in your daughter. Enough that he is on this ship to protect her from Mr. Wright. And he is always looking for promising investments. He seems the hands-off sort when it comes to the running of business. You might be able to work something out that involves him in investing while allowing Gwendolyn to run the mines once they are married." I clasped my hands together, half waiting for an outburst of some sort. Instead, I was met by silence.

"Do you really think she is interested in him? I don't want to push her towards another marriage unless she really wants it."

"If only my mother had felt the same way! I do believe she wants this union. But why don't you go ask her? Include her in your planning. It can only help you decide what is best," I said.

"You're right, Miss Porter. I need to talk to my daughter. But first, I would like to do something to thank you. You not only got my wife's jewels back, but you saved our family from disaster. There has to be some way I can thank you."

"Really, I don't want anything from you. That is, I want you to speak to your daughter and listen to her, that's thanks enough for me."

Mr. Wilcox looked surprised. "I must say, you have access to a mine of emeralds, and you just want me to listen to my daughter? I've never known someone to not ask for something for themselves. You are unique."

"I have heard that a time or two," I said with a smile.

"I won't have it. You deserve a reward. When we are off the ship, you must come to my office. I am going to give you a one percent share in my mine. It's not much, but the dividends should help you continue on your journey. I also insist you use our suite at The Standard Hotel in New Lankersham at no cost while you are there." Mr. Wilcox pulled out a pen and his card, and started writing on the back of it.

"I couldn't . . ." I didn't need a reward, or even want one. Society would have me turn all of it down, but I was about to disembark to live in a new country with no place to stay and no way to ensure my funds would last. I may not have wanted the reward, but it would be illogical to turn it down.

"I absolutely must insist. I have no idea what your plans are, but two women traveling alone need all the help they can get."

"If you insist, how can I say no to such a lovely offer? Thank you, your generosity is overwhelming." I took the card that Mr. Wilcox held out for me. On it were directions to his attorney's office and the address of the hotel. Lia and I now had a destination for the next leg of this adventure.

*   *   *

Chapter Twenty

New Lankersham, July 1, 1850

Dear Diary,

How wonderful today is! Lia and I have packed our bags after all our days at sea and will disembark any moment now. I am so excited to discover what this new world has in store for me. Granted, I will miss my new friends. I hope to stay in touch with Gwendolyn. I have a feeling the emerald mines will help me maintain a comfortable life under her stewardship. To think that Mr. Wilcox offered me a share in his company as a thank you! I pinched myself after it happened to make sure it was real; I never thought they would thank me in such a splendid way. It does make one think.

I will also miss the captain and his flirtation. It does make a lady feel special to have that kind of attention. Maybe I'll be on one of his ships again in the future. Who knows what will happen?

As for Mr. Rupert Holmes, I have a feeling we will see each other again. Maybe one day I'll figure out why he makes me feel, well . . . things. Things I don't understand. But until we meet again, I intend to do what I can to leave my mark on the world. Who am I kidding? If we meet again, he won't stop me from doing what I want, and hopefully, leaving the world a better place because of who I am.

*   *   *

"Can you believe it, Lia? We are about to disembark, and we are going to be in a new country, on a new continent, a new world for us! I cannot wait to explore and see all this new place has to offer." I spun around in our little room, my green skirts floating around me. My excitement could not, would not, be contained. Opening the door, I waltzed up the hallway.

Lia followed as I continued my happy dance. "Honoria, you are too much! Do you think the porter will be able to handle our bags?"

I stopped. "Yes, they can manage. And thank you for your fine needlework last night. I feel like my jewels are safe. Have I expressed properly how happy I am that I don't need to sell them yet?" I rubbed my hands down my bodice. Lia had sewn pockets into the waistband of my petticoats. Now all my jewelry was under layers of fabric, next to my person. I felt like the jewels were safe and not at all noticeable.

"I do feel like all of our things are much safer how they are packed. People keep talking about all the crazy things that happen in Eletharis and New Lankersham. I hope we are not set upon by pickpockets, or worse, hardened criminals." Lia twisted her hands together until she saw I noticed. She then stopped and wiped her palms down her skirts. Her fingers twitched like her nervous energy needed a way to escape.

"Come on, let's go to the walkway and watch what's happening on the dock." I grabbed her hand and dragged her outside to the railing. I stared out, taking in all the movement along the dock. Barrels were being hoisted and packed on wagons; fish were being thrown into crates filled with salt or ice. Women had stands set up and seemed to be selling food to anyone who stopped. The movement was constant, and the noise was like nothing I had ever heard before.

"Miss Porter, Miss Thompson, what do you think of the port here in New Lankersham?" Rupert Holmes stood beside me. He was so close to me that our arms almost touched. Butterflies took residence in my stomach and started a riot there.

"It's amazing; so much movement, like watching a ballet, except none of them are actually dancing. It's just people going about their daily business," I said, looking over at Mr. Holmes to find him watching me.

"Where will your journey take you next, Miss Porter?" he asked, maintaining eye contact.

His intense gaze was too much for me. My eyes dropped down to his mouth. I licked my lips, jerking my head away from him. "Mr. Wilcox has offered us use of his suite at The Standard Hotel for the foreseeable future. Lia and I will stay there while we discuss where we want to go after we explore New Lankersham."

"I think you will enjoy The Standard. It is in a very nice part of town. I hope Mr. Wilcox and his wife will help facilitate your entry into New Lankersham society. It is both similar and yet vastly different to what you are used to in Fintan."

"I don't know about going about in high society. I've had enough of those arbitrary standards. I want to experience something different here, something more meaningful." The breeze picked up, taking my words and my hairpins with it. "Oh dear, my hair!"

"Your hair is gorgeous floating in the breeze. But here, this will help keep it out of your way as you walk around town." Mr. Holmes took his bowler hat and put it on my head. "And I recommend giving society here a chance, make connections. And when you're done, come to Gaofar. Come find me." He slipped his card into the band of his hat that now rested on my head.

I watched as Mr. Holmes walked away, leaving me standing by the rail in stunned silence.

"What was that all about?" Lia asked.

"I don't know, Lia. I honestly don't know." My eyes followed him as he walked down the gangplank and strode into the crowd. I didn't look away until I could no longer make him out among all the others.

*   *   *

The Daring Adventures

of

Honoria Porter:

Part Two

New Lankersham

Chapter One

New Lankersham, September 15, 1850

Dear Diary,

It has been quite an experience through the last couple of months in New Lankersham. I've found my way into high society here. What amazes me is how different it is from Fintan and how much of it has stayed the same. Here, everyone has earned their money by having some involvement in trade or business. While there is this idea of "new money" and "old money," no one has a place because of a title, so the who's who of New Lankersham can change. One of the most interesting differences is how men with certain professions are sought after because they have a steady income. Back home, matchmaking mamas only look for a title.

Another interesting difference is how many women here are involved in politics, even though they have no say in them. Just like back home, women here are not allowed to vote, cannot hold certain professions, and will lose any property they own when they marry. Despite all that, women are out trying to garner attention for a ton of different issues. One, which I agree with wholeheartedly, is safe clothing for women. I read a story just the other day about a woman who got too close to the fireplace and caught on fire because of her crinolines. The poor woman suffered horrendous burns and did not survive the recovery process. Why are women wearing such hazardous fashions, skirts that flair out two-to-three feet from our body, so we aren't always aware of our clothing's distance to dangerous objects?

I'm also fascinated by the free love movement. It gives women so many more choices. The basic principle is everyone has the right to love who they want for as long as they want, whether it be forever or for a day. Also part of this movement is the principle that the institution of marriage needs to be rethought. Instead of a business transaction, it should be based on love and compatibility, and easily ended if one's feelings change. Some of the members of the movement like to call out how their opposition actually lives like they believe in free love while touting this moral high ground that implies free love is completely immoral. This famous preacher was all over the news, lambasting the free love concept, and turns out he's been having an affair for months. He's not even practicing the fidelity he claims we all should strive for.

*   *   *

My back had started hurting so long ago that I couldn't remember a time when it hadn't been in pain, and now my legs were cramping from holding this ridiculous position for so long. If I had known modeling for a painter would be so uncomfortable, I never would have said yes. I'll admit, Pierre's flattery had turned my head, and I hadn't even thought of the many consequences when he asked me to be his muse. Now that I knew such consequences included pain in areas I didn't even know could ache, I would think twice before agreeing to an artist's whims again.

At the moment, I was stuck keeping my promise, which somehow included me lounging on a divan in my corset and petticoat with a luxurious green velvet robe hanging off my shoulders, barely closed in front, and my red hair tumbling down my back in a riot of curls. I didn't even have shoes on, and Pierre insisted my toes show from underneath my petticoats and robe. I never would have thought bare feet would make something seem almost intimate, but for some reason, it did.

"Ah, Honoria, you have moved. I beg of you to not do so again. The painting will not be right if you continue to move." Pierre continued to stare at the canvas as he brushed more paint onto it.

I wanted to roll my eyes. I was a living, breathing person, not an inanimate object. However, I refrained.

"I could really use a respite, and maybe some tea—or something a little stronger. The position you've placed me in may look comfortable, but it is not, and hasn't been for hours." I'm sure I sounded like a spoiled child, but I was in pain and no longer happy about it.

"My beauty, your perfection is natural, but to capture it takes time. Just a little longer, my sweet." Pierre looked around his canvas, his eyes pleading with me.

"Fine, Pierre, I will continue to pose for you. For now. But I want to see your painting soon. It's hard to hold this position for hours and not see your progress." I settled back into a position no woman would ever choose to lounge in.

"Ah yes, that is it." Pierre walked over and fixed my hair. "There, now it looks like fire cascading down your back. Everything—it is perfection."

I noticed the shadows in the room lengthen as Pierre continued to paint. He did not look at me so much as a woman than an inspiration for his art—I might as well have been a fruit bowl—until I heard a door creak open.

"Oh no! You must leave at once." Pierre looked up at me, eyes wide with horror. "My wife, she is here."

"Pierre, you told me she knew I was here. That she didn't mind. And she shouldn't mind. Nothing untoward is happening here." I stood, crossing my arms so I felt less exposed.

Pierre shuffled his feet. "I lied. I'm sorry it has come to this. Your beauty inspired me, but she would never have approved. And she didn't when I asked as you requested. Now go, quickly, quickly." Pierre tossed my gown and shoes out the window before I could stop him.

"Have you lost your mind! Why would you throw my things out the window?" I felt my face heating up with rage. "What do you mean, you lied?"

I pulled the green robe on, crossing my arms as I stood in front of Pierre. To say I was not happy would be an understatement. I only said yes to sitting for Pierre after he promised me his wife had agreed to it. It was the only consequence I had considered when embarking on this little adventure.

"I had to capture your beauty and Celeste didn't understand. Even after I told her it was just a sitting, nothing more," Pierre paced the room, cleaning up his painting supplies as he did so.

"Is there any reason she would doubt you?" I asked.

"I may have had a few indiscretions with my muses in the past." Pierre shrugged as if to dismiss the importance of his past actions.

"No wonder she doesn't trust you. Why should she trust you?" I said, turning to pace the room.

"Now, Miss Porter, Honoria, please. Can you please go?" He gestured to the window.

I sighed. I guessed it was time for me to go out the window. As angry as I was at Pierre, I didn't want to cause his poor wife any distress. So I shimmied out the second-story window onto the narrow ledge. I had hoped for an outdoor stairwell or a ladder, but I was out of luck. I was going to have to jump and hope nothing ended up broken. With a small prayer, I stepped off the ledge.

"Oof." I heard a man grunt as I felt a pair of muscular arms wrap around me. I looked up into the most crystal-clear blue eyes I've ever seen in my life. "I heard Eletharis was the land of the plenty, but I hadn't expected gorgeous women to fall from the sky."

The man with the stunning eyes set me on my feet, taking in my lack of shoes. I blushed. The man collected my dress and shoes from the ground and handed them to me.

"Reece Farrows, at your service," he said with a gallant bow.

I took my things from him and did the only thing a self-respecting woman could do—ran.

*   *   *

Chapter Two

New Lankersham, September 16, 1850

Dear Diary,

One would think after a day like yesterday, I would take a day to rest and compose myself. However, there is no rest for the . . . well, I'm not exactly wicked, but I don't feel like my actions of late have shown me in the best light. Although, why should I be the one to feel shame? I told Pierre I would only pose for him if he asked his wife and she was okay with it. He's the one who lied to both of us. He should be the one with this distasteful feeling of guilt. Not me; I was deceived. And while I may not be completely innocent, I definitely am a victim of Pierre's lies. And I didn't even get to see the painting.

Oh well, I must move on. Tonight, I'm going to the symphony with my dear friend Frederika and, of course, Lia. Rika is still young, but she has made quite the name for herself as the arbiter of high society. I wouldn't be surprised if she holds New Lankersham in her iron fist for decades to come. Rika's father plans on leaving her a fortune, and her fiancé, Ambrose Austin Jacobs, has agreed that all the money will be Rika's to do with as she pleases. Can you even imagine? I know nothing like this would occur back in Fintan. But Mr. Jacobs has a fortune of his own; he's just so-called new money. Where Rika's family, the Schumann's, have been wealthy forever. Mr. Schumann has his money in so many different ventures—I can only aspire to be like him.

*   *   *

"Oh Lia, you wouldn't even believe it." I turned in my chair to face her, causing her to drop a half dozen hairpins. "I'm so sorry." My hair fell in complete disarray when I dropped to my knees to pick up the pins. I swear, if Lia was back in Fintan, she would have left me by now.

Lia sighed. "Honoria, you have to stay still while I fix your hair. Miss Frederika Wylie Schumann will be here soon, and you are nowhere near ready to head out. You know how she hates to wait."

I picked up the last of the hair pins and sat back into my chair. Lia wasn't wrong, but that didn't mean I had to like it. She had been out and about all day, so I hadn't told her about my misadventures with Pierre. It was more fun for me when I could see her reactions to whatever outrageous thing I had done.

"Fine, but you must let me see you in the mirror as I tell my story. I promise no more quick movements if you do."

"Very well, what is it I won't believe this time?" Lia loved my antics, even if she pretended to be exasperated by them the majority of the time.

"As I was saying, there I was posing for Pierre, in nothing but my undergarments and a robe, when we hear a door shut. Pierre loses his mind and throws my dress and shoes out the window, insisting I follow them so his wife doesn't find me."

"I told you he was no good. Figures he couldn't even do the one thing that you asked for: get permission from his wife." Lia rolled her eyes at his actions.

"I know. That's the only thing I asked for. And he lied to me, telling me she was fine with it. He made me so angry. Anyway, I really didn't see another way out, so I go out the window. Except there's nothing there to help me down. I have to jump. So, I give a short prayer and I leap off the wall and land in the arms of a man with the most stunning blue eyes I've ever seen. He sets me down and introduces himself, but I cannot respond. So, I grabbed my things, and I ran."

"What are you going to do if you see this man again?" Lia asked, her eyes wide.

"Honestly, Lia, I don't know. We can always hope I won't ever see him again," I said.

*   *   *

"Is that a new gown, Honoria?" Frederika Wylie Schumann asked as we walked into the Schumann Opera House. Yes—her father had paid for the building to be built, and because of our friendship, Lia and I had access to the best box seats in town. It was quite delightful.

"It is. I decided after putting up with the grueling heat of summer, something I've never experienced before that Lia and I both deserved a new gown. I couldn't help but get this emerald green silk. It's a bit passé to have a signature color, but I do love how the green looks on me. I always feel like my hair looks shinier and my eyes sparkle more," I said with a coy smile. "Don't you think Lia looks positively angelic in that icy blue? She insisted she didn't need a new dress, but I would not be deterred.”

“She does look lovely as well. However, nothing can compare to your vivaciousness. All eyes will be on our box tonight because you are sitting there. I can't wait to introduce you to everyone, including the conductor, Daniel Rochester. He writes the most whimsical music. I am certain you will love it, Honoria.”

Rika grabbed my arm, almost dragging me to her box. I looked back to see Lia following at a more sedate pace. She gave a little shrug, then nodded, letting me know she was fine making her way to our seats.

I glanced around the wonderfully ornate building. The rich, red velvet carpet covering the marble tile was stunning against the paneled walls. Everything about the building was the very definition of decadent.

Rika practically burst through the door to her box when we arrived, barely giving me time to hide behind her as I saw the man from last night turn. What was his name? Oh yes, Reece Farrows.

Rika took a step back as I planted myself outside the door. “I'm sorry, Rika, I need to go to the retiring room. I'm afraid I stepped on my hem and must have Lia fix it immediately.”

“Of course.” Rika waved me away as she turned to

her guest.

I hurried back to Lia. Grabbing her by the arm, I pulled her away from our seats.

"He's here," I whispered, my face heating up. I was certain to be bright red in an instant.

"Who's here, Honoria? Are you alright? You look quite flushed." Lia asked as I burst into the retiring room, causing the handful of ladies in there to scurry out. I must have been quite the sight at the moment.

"The man that caught me last night, he's a guest of Rika's. What am I going to do?" I paced the length of the room, trying to decide on the best course of action.

"Do you want to leave? I can call us a cab," Lia offered.

"It would be a shame to miss Daniel Rochester. He's supposed to have a unique way of expressing himself in music. He's the future of orchestra." I stopped pacing. I was being dramatic. "You know what, Lia, I'll just brave it out. What's the absolute worst that can happen? My character may be ruined, but we can just leave town if it is. It wouldn't be the first time." I was referring to how the two of us ended up in Eletharis, running away from the marriage my mother desperately sought and manipulated. I was not just in a new town, but a whole new country, with only my lady's maid as a companion. The two of us had done well so far. There was nothing to it. I had to continue as I started: daring and unconventional in all things.

"I'm sure you can handle it. You have a way of charming gentlemen. I doubt this man, whoever he is, will be immune." Lia laughed as we both turned to leave the retiring room.

*   *   *

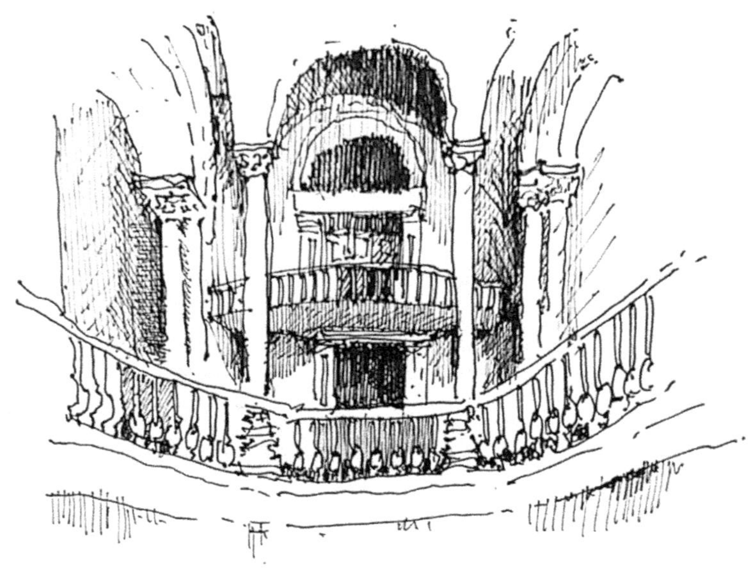

Chapter Three

New Lankersham, September 16, 1850

Dear Diary,

I learned a few things at the symphony tonight, It was
such an intriguing night that I'm writing now, as soon as I
settled in for the night instead of tomorrow morning. First,
business in New Lankersham is cutthroat. There is no
pretense of gentle behavior. I hate to think how far a person
would go to make a deal happen. I could definitely see the
employ of extortion, but I wonder if it could go even further
than that. Second, Reece Farrows is such a businessman.
The things I overheard . . . as a lady I cannot repeat them;
although, when has that ever stopped me before? And third,
he may be a cutthroat businessman, but Mr. Farrows has

stunning blue eyes, a fine form, and presents himself as if he is actually a gentleman.

*   *   *

"This is a mistake, Lia. What was I thinking, trying to brazen it out? He's going to tell someone that he knows me. And then it will get out I was parading around town in my undergarments."

Panic was setting in. I wasn't sure if I would be able to handle judgment from my newfound friends. It had been different before. I knew I was leaving and had a plan. However, I didn't have an escape plan set in place yet. If nothing else, this situation illustrated how much I would always need to have a way out planned. Something to think about as soon as tonight was over.

Lia looked over at me and rolled her eyes. She didn't appreciate my dramatics. "I'm sure this man is a gentleman and will keep his mouth shut in front of others. Knowing you, you'll find another activity for his mouth when it's just the two of you."

I gasped. "Lia, I am shocked at your suggestion."

"Do you deny it?" Lia raised her fair eyebrow.

"No, I'm just shocked that you would suggest it." I giggled.

Lia and I turned down the hall that led to Rika's box

seats. Just outside the door, two men looked to be in a heated conversation, arms flailing, chests puffed. It looked like if they weren't standing in an opera house they would come to blows despite their fancy suits. I gestured for Lia to stop as I slipped into an alcove, out of sight of the two men, pulling Lia in with me. Carefully, I snuck to the edge of the alcove, careful to stay hidden. I was a nosey sort and really wanted to know what they were arguing about.

"Forget about it, Reece. There's nothing you can say to me that would convince me to sell you my railroad. I have no interest in being part of the New Lankersham Central Railroad system," an unknown man said, apparently talking to the man from last night.

"Really, William, why are you being so stubborn? I'm not even asking you to sell it to us anymore. I just want to use your piece of track along the river that's essential to connect upper and lower New Lankersham. Can we not come to an agreement where you will accept tickets sold by the New Lankersham Central Railroad, and I pay out on a monthly basis or on any basis you think is fair?" My savior argued. It seemed like a sensible argument to me. More and more business was done in lower New Lankersham, with homes being built on the upper side.

"It's my land and I will do what I want with it," the

man called William said.

"I understand it's your land. That being said, you will come to regret not participating in this venture."

"Why does that sound like a threat?" William said.

I was about to step out of the alcove when I heard the thud of footsteps on the carpet. Instead of exiting, I took a half-step back, so Lia and I remained unseen. I held my hand up so Lia stayed where she was.

"I'd be careful, Mr. Waring, an attitude like that is going to see that you're taken care of," Reece called after the man walking away.

After a moment passed, I looked out of our hiding place. The hall was empty. I stepped out, pulling Lia with me.

"What was that all about, Honoria?"

"I have no idea, but neither man sounded happy with the other. One of them was the man from last night." I brushed my hands down my skirts, preparing to enter our box. "Let's take our seats and discuss this later."

Lia sighed, but she followed me into the box. Rika looked up with a smile and a questioning gaze. I nodded, letting her know my minor mishap had been fixed for the moment. She didn't need to know the truth, at least not yet. To her right was Rika's fiancé, Ambrose Austen Jacobs.

Next to him was Reece Farrows. On Rika's left were two empty chairs, I assumed, for Lia and myself. Behind our row were two seats. In one sat a lady, Ava Waring. I believed I had met her at another of Rika's gatherings. And if seated in here was Mrs. Waring, the man who stormed away could only be her husband and railroad owner, William Waring.

"Ambrose, you must introduce me to these two lovely ladies. I do not believe I've had the pleasure of meeting them yet. Are they new in town?" Reece stood and made his way the short distance across the balcony.

"They arrived a couple months ago. This is Miss Honoria Porter and her companion, Lia Thompson." Ambrose gestured towards Lia and me.

"And you are?" I asked with a raise of my eyebrow, daring him to say something about last night.

"Reece Farrows, at your service," he said with a slight bow, then rising with a smirk and a twinkle in his blue eyes.

"I do believe the musicians are about to start. You should take your seat."

"Of course, Miss Porter." He took my hand in his and raised it to his lips, turning it over at the last moment to place a kiss on the inside of my wrist. I shivered; I was always drawn in by a man who was an incorrigible flirt, and it appeared there was one standing right in front of me.

I sat down as the music roared to life. Everything I had heard about Daniel Rochester was true. I forgot about all my concerns as the whimsical notes washed over me.

* * *

Chapter Four

New Lankersham, September 18, 1850

Dear Diary,

Yesterday I decided it was a day to just lounge around. Thankfully, I hadn't made any plans, and no one called on us. If they had, I think I would have had them turned away. I couldn't imagine going out again after the past few days. Instead, I curled up with a book and lounged around all day.

Today is a new day, and Ambrose has invited us to watch his horse, Serendipity, race for the first time. Incidentally, this is my first time watching a horse race, and I am beside myself with excitement.

*   *   *

"Lia, we have to hurry. The train to Sandison Downs is supposed to be at the station in thirty minutes. Rika and Ambrose will be at our stop to take us to the track." I said as if Lia was the one that was causing the delay.

"I'm ready, Honoria. I even have your hat and gloves here. We can leave whenever you're ready." Lia held out my accessories.

I grabbed a hat pin from my vanity and pinned my hat. "Let's go, there's no time to waste."

Lia laughed as I took the gloves from her and ran down the stairs of our hotel, there was not time to wait for the lift today. I still can't believe how lucky we were to have a nice place to stay in the city at no cost. I was so thankful that the Wilcoxes had insisted we stay here for as long as we liked after the incident on the ship.

The hotel was also close to the train station. As worried as I was about being late, Lia and I actually had a decent amount of time to get to the station. I was sure we would have at least a few minutes to spare. I didn't enjoy relying on someone or something else to get me to places on time—it took away a level of control that I very much enjoyed having—but the train was a financially prudent way to get about town.

The muggy summer heat was shifting into the brisk weather one expects in autumn, making the walk to the station the most pleasant it had ever been. For the first time, I stood on the platform and didn't need to use my fan to dry the unladylike glisten that always appeared from the walk.

"Miss Porter, what a surprise to see you again so soon," I heard a recognizable male voice say. I turned to see Reece Farrows tilting his hat to Lia, who blushed prettily.

"Mr. Farrows, where are you off to this fine day?" I gave him a coy smile and fluttered my eyelashes a little. I enjoyed flirting with others almost as much as I enjoyed when someone flirted with me.

"Sandison Downs, of course. I couldn't miss Serendipity's first race."

"How fortuitous! Lia and I are headed there as well. Mr. Jacobs was going on the other day about his new horse. I don't think I've ever seen anyone quite as excited about an animal as he was."

The piercing whistle of the train interrupted our conversation as the line of cars pulled into the station.

"I'm sure you will find many such gentlemen at the tracks today. Everyone is excited about the fall races and checking out the new quarter horses that are making their debut today, Serendipity being one of them." Mr. Farrows held an arm to Lia and me. The discussion continued as we boarded the train.

"Are you one such gentleman, Mr. Farrows?" I asked.

"I'm afraid to admit I am not. What you see around you is my obsession. I cannot wait to make cross-country travel affordable to everyone. It's going to change the world we live in. It's already changed New Lankersham considerably." Mr. Farrows pointed to different details on the car, from the wood-paneled and papered walls to the velvet-covered bench seating. Everything he pointed to whispered elegance and luxury. Mr. Farrows stopped inside the next car. "I believe your seats are in here."

I looked around, taking in the wood paneling and green velvet that ensconced us. Lia did the same beside me. A man in livery appeared in front of the three of us.

"Champagne," he offered.

I glanced over at Mr. Farrows. "You must be mistaken. I know we did not pay for such luxury today."

Lia jabbed me with her elbow. I turned to glare at her. Instead, I saw her holding a glass of champagne, having already accepted Mr. Farrows's hospitality.

"It's my railway, so I decided you should travel with me in style. This is my private car." Mr. Farrows stepped farther into the car with a sweeping gesture, allowing Lia and me to take in all the subtle details as we walked farther in. It reminded me of the dining room of the ship from Brythion, but on a much smaller scale. The seats looked plush and inviting. There was a small station for the servers to prepare drinks, maybe more, and the windows were large, allowing anyone in the train car to take in views of the city or countryside, whatever it happened to be.

"I didn't know this was your railway. From what I've seen, it appears you take great pride in your business. Do you have any plans to expand?" I asked, thinking of the conversation I had overheard at the symphony.

"I do. I want to have one rail company combine all the different railways in New Lankersham. Connecting ones that don't connect so that a person can travel anywhere in the city on one ticket."

"That's a very logical idea; I can't see why anyone would oppose it."

"You would be surprised, Miss Porter. At the moment, there are four individuals that own railways in the area. Two of the others have agreed to sell to me outright. The last owner is not interested, but his line runs up and down the river. Without it, the combining of our companies is somewhat pointless." Mr. Farrows took off his hat and handed it to one of the servers. "Enough talk of business. Enjoy the ride to Sandison Downs."

Mr. Farrows left Lia and me on our own for the ride down. I must admit to a tinge of disappointment as he left to check on the other cars. It would have been a much more entertaining ride if I had been able to continue our flirtation. Instead, Lia and I were left to entertain ourselves.

"Lia, what do you think of Mr. Farrows?"

Lia accepted another glass of champagne before turning to me. "I would say that he is friendly and respectful. At least, that's what he presents to the public. He hasn't even alluded to your fall into his arms. I don't believe he is faking his demeanor at all. He also has excellent taste in champagne." She raised her glass towards me.

"I guess I should partake. It would be silly of me to ignore such hospitality. But Lia, remember we have an entire day at the racetrack after this. There's no time to nap beforehand." I tried to give her a stern look; however, I was anything but stern. On the ship, a couple of glasses of champagne were enough to send Lia to sleep for hours. There was no time for that today.

Lia pouted. "I will finish this one and have no more. I wouldn't want to ruin anyone's fun because bubbles make me sleepy."

It wasn't long before the combination of bubbles and the rocking of the train put Lia to sleep. Instead of waking her, I watched the scenery go by until Mr. Farrows entered the car. I elbowed Lia to wake her up before he walked over to our seats.

"What, Honoria?" she said, her voice thick with sleep.

"We are almost there, and Mr. Farrows is back to escort us," I whispered.

"Oh," she said. She tried to rub her eyes without drawing attention to the fact she had been sleeping.

"Miss Porter, Miss Thompson, we are almost at our destination. If you will allow it, I would love to escort you off the train."

"Why thank you, Mr. Farrows. We would be delighted. This is all new to us. I can't wait to see the horses race." I stood, ignoring his proffered arm. Instead, I made my way towards the exit on my own and waited for the train to come to a complete stop.

Rika and her fiancé, Ambrose, were waiting on the platform for us. Waving at them, I stepped off the train. Mr. Farrows and Lia were right behind me.

"I'm so excited to see the race, Mr. Jacobs. What do you think her chances are of winning?" I asked.

"This is her first formal race, so I expect her to do well, but would be surprised if she won. You're still in for a treat though. There's nothing like a good horse race. Mr. Waring and his wife as well as Daniel Rochester are already at the track. If we hurry, I can introduce you to Serendipity and her jockey, Toby MacGregor before the race," Ambrose said, hurrying us down the platform and out of the station.

"Ambrose, I'll meet you there. I have a carriage here and might need to leave early," Mr. Farrows said as he walked towards a high-sprung carriage with two gorgeous chestnuts harnessed in front.

"Of course, of course. See you at the tracks, Reece." Ambrose escorted us to his lovely open carriage. It was a perfect day to be out and about.

It seemed we stopped at our destination almost before the trip began. A footman helped Lia, Rika, and me down, ensuring that we did not trip and fall on the carriage steps.

Ambrose alighted. "Rika, dear, give me a moment and then follow with everyone. I want to make sure Serendipity is ready for company."

"Of course, Ambrose. Go take care of your horse." Rika waved him away. "Ambrose is over the moon that everyone showed up to see his new horse. I think he's more excited for people to meet her than he's ever been about introducing me. Let's find the others and then head over." Rika's tinkling laugh drifted as the breeze picked up.

I grabbed my hat as the wind tugged at it. My hair never cooperated in anything but the politest of weather. Hopefully, the breeze would calm down.

"Oh there, Mr. Rochester, Mrs. Waring! You must come to see Serendipity. Ambrose would be devastated if you missed out. Mrs. Waring, where's your husband?" Rika asked.

She waved dismissively. "He left to go to the stables a while ago. You know how he is. An idea enters his head and he must act on it immediately."

"Then we will just have to find him along the way." Rika directed us towards the stables, taking Mr. Rochester by the arm. Mrs. Waring took his other arm; Lia and I followed directly behind them.

The group arrived at the stables just as Reece and Ambrose did. However, Mr. Waring was nowhere in sight.

Ambrose stepped in front of the stall door. "Here she is, my Serendipity, and her jockey, Mr. MacGregor."

I had already wandered off to the next stall. There was a puddle of something right under the stall door. It didn't look right. When I approached, no horse came forward, so I opened the gate. Something brushed across the front of my dress before landing on the ground with a thud. I looked down to see the vacant eyes of Mr. William Waring staring at me. My eyes moved from Mr. Waring to my skirts to see the red stain running down the front of them. I screamed. I had just been touched by a dead man.

*   *   *

Chapter Five

New Lankersham, September 18, 1850

Dear Diary,

I don't even know where to start. At least no one is accusing me of the crime this time. Is that too shallow of a thought to have after finding a dead body? It probably is, but I'm a little wary after my experience on the ship.

I can't believe Mr. Waring is dead. I just saw him the other night at the symphony arguing with Reece Farrows. It makes me wonder . . .

*   *   *

I stood there, not knowing what to do. I had never been near a dead body before, much less had one fall right on me. Somewhere, I heard another woman wailing. I assumed it was Mrs. Waring. She did have a reason to express herself in a dramatic way, an excellent reason. After all, it was her husband lying on the ground at my feet.

"What is going on here?" a man asked.

I looked up to see someone I did not recognize running his hand through his sandy blond hair. I watched as his gray eyes darted from the body at my feet, to me, then to Mrs. Waring. I glanced over at my friends; it appeared that Lia and I were the only two people who didn't recognize the newcomer.

"Mayor Beaufort, we are in desperate need of a government official. It is fortuitous you are here," Rika said as she grabbed the man's arm and escorted him over to where I was standing. I could tell she was doing all she could to avert her eyes from the ground, avoiding the inevitable acknowledgment of what had happened, all while doing what she could to handle the matter. It was clear she would control this city eventually by her ability to handle the matter at hand. I was impressed.

"I say, has anyone sent for the police?" Mayor Beaufort asked.

"Not yet, Honoria discovered the body just a few moments ago," Rika said as she took my arm and moved me away from the body.

"Of course, that's understandable." Mayor Beaufort snapped his fingers to gain the attention of a young man. He then waved him away, sending the young man scurrying off. I assumed to go get an officer to investigate. "Someone let them know the race needs to be postponed. We can't very well go on as normal when a man has been murdered."

I looked over at Mr. Waring. It was pretty obvious the man had been killed by having his head bashed in, which also explained all the blood on my dress.

I gasped.

Only two nights ago, I had overheard him arguing with Mr. Farrows over Mr. Waring's railroad.

"Is everything okay, Miss . . .?" the mayor asked. He had zeroed in on me after sending off his assistant to handle matters.

"Porter, Honoria Porter," I responded. "I'm as fine as anyone can be having just discovered a dead body."

"You do seem rather composed, except for a moment ago. What were you thinking about just now?" Mayor Beaufort said.

Bloody hell, he thought I wasn't acting like a lady because I was calm. I should probably be more upset. It took a moment for me to decide what my best course of action was. I really didn't want to draw the attention of any government official. So I did the one thing everyone would expect of a young, impressionable lady—I fainted.

"Oh my, Honoria," I heard Lia exclaim from behind my closed eyes. I waited until I felt her at my side before I dared to peek out.

"Get me out of here," I said through gritted teeth as Lia leaned over me, blocking my face from view.

"Smelling salts. Does anyone have smelling salts?" Lia looked around frantically. Someone must have offered her some, because next thing I knew, I was breathing in that awful odor.

I spluttered and coughed. "What happened?" I looked around like I was confused.

"You fainted, Honoria. Why don't I find you a spot where you can compose yourself?" Rika said.

Lia helped me off the ground. I saw Ambrose, Reece, Toby, and Daniel all talking to a man in a uniform. The mayor was next to Mrs. Waring. I wondered if any of them had killed Mr. Waring.

*　　*　　*

"Lia, thank you so much. If I hadn't done something, it felt like I was going to be a suspect, and I didn't want to go through that again," I said as soon as Rika left the room.

"It would have been extremely strange for anyone to suspect you. I mean, you barely know Mr. Waring. Why would you have wanted him dead? And could you even hit him over the head with that much force?"

"You're right, but the mayor was judging me, and if I didn't do something appropriately feminine, the others would have judged me as well." My brain was whirling with everything I knew about Mr. Waring, which admittedly wasn't much. "Do you think his death has anything to do with the railroad deal he refused to be a part of? Mr. Farrows practically threatened him the other night. And he wasn't super happy about him this morning either." I stood so I could pace the room, the heels of my boots marking each time my foot came down on the oak floor.

"I can't believe that he would have anything to do with something so sordid. He has been such a gentleman, especially to you, after, well, you know." Lia ran her hands over the rich brocade of the sofa.

"Does being a gentleman in certain circumstances mean you are a gentleman in all of them? You heard him at the opera house. It sounded like he was threatening Mr. Waring." I stopped and took in the room around me. "Where are we? This room doesn't look like something you would find at a racetrack."

"Someone that Rika knows. It's their home. Rika left you a shawl to cover the . . . stain." Lia shuddered when she glanced at the dried blood on my dress.

"That's good. I would hate to draw attention to myself for the wrong reasons. And this dress has seen better days," I said, laughing. Just the thought of me trying not to draw attention to myself made it hard not to laugh uncontrollably. But then I thought of Mr. Waring, and I stopped midlaugh. "I want to go back, look at the stall where I found Mr. Waring. Maybe there's something there that will help us figure out who killed him."

"Why? There's no need for you to figure out who killed him. Don't you think it would be best to just let the men hired to investigate do their job?"

"I'm worried about Rika. The other night two of Ambrose's friends argued and now one of them is dead. What if he has surrounded himself with unsavory people. I don't want to see her hurt because of who her fiancé associates with." I tied the shawl around my skirt to hide the hideous stain running down the front of it. Looking over at Lia, I asked, "Are you coming?"

She huffed, but I heard her grab her things as I headed to the door. I was intent on solving this murder.

*   *   *

Chapter Six

New Lankersham, September 18, 1850

Dear Diary,

I never would have thought a day at the races could turn into what it did. Concern for my dear friend, as well as insatiable curiosity had me scrounging around a horse stall next to the recently departed.

*　　*　　*

The smell of hay wafted towards me as I stood outside the horse stall that housed Mr. Waring's body. It was strangely quiet. The police weren't there at the moment, but I didn't know how long they would be gone. I looked around to ensure the mayor wasn't on his way back before opening the stall door. Taking a deep breath, I pushed my way through. Mr. Waring was lying on his back, half covered with a horse blanket. It didn't seem like the most dignified way to leave a body, but I doubted anyone was expecting a dead body would turn up at the races.

"What are you looking for, Honoria?" Lia asked as she peaked over the stall door. I turned back to see her shiver and look away. It was clear that Lia was not comfortable being near the body.

"I don't know, Lia. Something that points to someone. I'm hoping I recognize a clue when I find one. If not, this is a waste of time. Why don't you stand out there and keep an eye out? Let me know when the mayor or one of his police officers are on their way back. I can't believe they just left the place unguarded."

The smell of the stall shifted from hay to cut wood as I moved closer to Mr. Waring. His head was caved in on the top right side as if someone had swung something with a downward curve and struck him. I stared a moment, unsure where to look. Confused that I was taking in this scene with such calm. It took a moment, but I shrugged away any concerns I had about whether my reactions were appropriate. Instead, I bent down and examined the body closer. Below the neck nothing was out of place, except for the dust on his clothing.

Wait—was there something clenched in his fist? I bent over to get a closer look. There was a paper in his hand. Why was he holding a paper? Could it have something to do with his murder? It took a moment to pry it from his fingers, especially without ripping it. The dead man's grip was strangely tight. I carefully unfolded the paper to find a note on it.

We need to meet, finish our conversation from the other night. To show there are no hard feelings, bet on Symphony in the second race. She'll have a little extra pep in her step today. Maybe you'll consider us even after the race.

"What is going on here?" I asked the empty stall.

I got back to my feet, looked around a little more, but didn't find anything else that looked important. I had hoped to see something that looked like it could have been the murder weapon, but the killer must have discarded it somewhere else. It was not in the stall as far as I could tell.

"Honoria, it's time to leave now. The mayor and a couple of policemen are headed our way," Lia said from outside the stables through clenched teeth.

Noting the urgency in her tone, I hurried out, careful to leave everything the way I found it. I grabbed Lia's arm and dragged her over to Serendipity's stall. The horse came to the front at our arrival, suggesting Lia and I had spent more time making friends with Serendipity than we actually had.

"Miss Porter, I was just on my way to see you. I hope you have recovered from . . . earlier," Mayor Beaufort said.

"As much as to be expected. Spending time with Serendipity here has helped tremendously. Don't you find animals to have a calming presence?" I asked as I stroked the horse's head.

"I . . . ah!" Mayor Beaufort swatted away a fly buzzing around his face and sighed. "Of course, such a calming presence." It was clear he didn't agree, but he was too polite to contradict a lady.

"You mentioned you wanted to see me?" I questioned with wide eyes. Earlier, the mayor had given the distinct impression he believed ladies acted a certain acceptable way. It had always been my experience that the more I played into that, the less they took note of me. There was something I didn't quite like about Mayor Beaufort. I wasn't sure if it was because I was suspicious of everyone at the moment or if there was truly something about him, but one could never be too careful.

"Yes, I was wondering, that is . . ." He swiped his

hand through his hair. It seemed to be a nervous gesture of sorts. "I hate to bring up today's unpleasantness. But I was hoping you could tell me what happened when you discovered Mr. Waring's body."

"There isn't really much to tell. There was a dark puddle on the ground in the stall next to Serendipity's, and I went to see what it was. The stall was empty, no horse, so I opened the gate, and well, you know the rest." I took my handkerchief out of my reticule and dabbed my eyes with it.

"Did you know Mr. Waring?"

"I had met his wife a few times, most recently we were guests of Miss Wylie Schumann and Mr. Jacobs at the Opera House. It was my first-time meeting Mr. Waring. We were there to see Daniel Rochester's orchestra."

"Ah, yes. I do believe I saw you there. That is to say, I saw you in the Schumanns' box."

"How unfortunate that we did not meet, Mayor Beaufort." I glanced over at Lia, trying to make eye contact. She needed to know what I found so I could make sense of it. Especially now; it seemed everyone here today was at the symphony the other night.

"Did you see anyone around the stall as you walked up?"

"What?" I shook my head to clear my thoughts. "No,

I didn't. I believe Ambrose was at Serendipity's stall. Rika, Mrs. Waring, Lia, Mr. Rochester, and I walked together to the area to meet the horse. Mr. Farrows was already with Ambrose when we got there. At least, I believe he was."

"Thank you, Miss Porter. Your cooperation has been invaluable. Now if I can just find Symphony and figure out why she wasn't in her stall," the mayor muttered.

"There's a horse named Symphony racing today? And she's missing?"

*   *   *

Chapter Seven

New Lankersham, September 19, 1850

Dear Diary,

I can't believe that a horse is missing. Why has no one mentioned it? Who owns the horse? Is the person who owns the horse the killer? Does that even make any sense? Then there was the note. It reminded me of the argument that Mr. Farrows and Mr. Waring had at the opera house. But why would he suggest betting on the horse that was missing? He hadn't mentioned being all that interested in horse racing. And what was the whole thing about "being even"? Mr. Farrows didn't seem to owe Mr. Waring anything. No one owes Mr. Waring anything anymore.

*   *   *

"I don't understand, Lia. There's a horse missing. A *horse*. No one has mentioned a missing horse." I paced across the sitting room in our hotel suite, the crinoline of my skirts rustling with every step I took.

"There was a murder. A horse doesn't seem that important in light of a dead body." Lia easily explained the lack of discussion away with a wave of her hand.

"You're right. It was probably just overlooked with everything else going on. It's still really strange." I shrugged, then flopped onto the divan. "I wonder how one goes about solving a murder? Where should I start?"

"First, I don't know why you feel the need to solve it at all. Second, shouldn't you start by analyzing the facts, just like you did on the ship?"

"But what are the facts, Lia? I don't know what we know other than that Mr. Waring is dead." Sitting still was too difficult. I stood; pacing always helped me think.

"Start with everyone we know who was at the opera house the other night. At least that's where I would start. That way, we can create a suspect list."

"You're a genius, Lia. I don't know what I would do without you." I stopped in the middle of the room and counted off everyone that was a suspect on my hand. "Okay, well, we know Mr. Farrows was there, as were Rika and Ambrose. Oh, and Daniel Rochester. We all saw him up on stage. Is there anyone else?" My feet insisted I move, so once again, the staccato sound of my heels hitting the floor filled the room.

"I think the mayor said he was there the other night. He mentioned seeing you there."

I stopped pacing and stared at Lia. "You're right. He did say that. That means the only person not there that we met yesterday was the jockey."

A knock on the door to our hotel suite interrupted my musings on potential suspects. The click of my heels on the marble floor echoed throughout the sitting room until I stopped in front of the door.

"Yes," I said as I opened the door. In front of me was a handsome, uniformed bellhop holding a card on a silver platter. It was very showy and a bit excessive in my mind, but the hotel was working on attracting a very specific type of guest. Thankfully, Lia and I fit right in because of our Brythionite upbringing.

"There is someone here to see you, Miss Porter."

"Thank you." I took the calling card from the plate. It was from Rika. Maybe she can help shed some light on all the going ons from the past few days. "Can you please send her up?"

"Very well. Good day, Miss Porter."

I closed the door as the bellhop turned and left. "It seems Rika has stopped by for a visit."

"Oh dear, I'm not dressed for her company." Lia looked down at her thin cotton dressing gown. The two of us had developed a bit of a pattern on the boat ride over. Lia enjoyed sleeping in. I had a habit of getting up at an unfashionable hour. I had learned the art of dressing myself during our initial travels, while Lia had learned the art of town hours. Sometimes I was envious of her ability to sleep once the sun was up.

"Go change; I know you will feel more comfortable if you do. Even though it's unnecessary. I don't think Rika would notice anything amiss, and if she did, her manners are polished enough that she would never say anything."

"You may be right, but I think she still views me as a servant and finds your insistence on bringing me along with you to everything off-putting," Lia said as she scurried to her room and behind the dressing screen. She threw the gown over the top of the screen and grabbed her corset. I could hear her struggles, but I knew from experience she would not accept my help. I stood inside the door as she grabbed her crinolines and a blue plaid dress. It seemed like mere moments before she was walking towards me dressed for the day.

"You look lovely, and I think most of the time you overthink when it comes to what others are thinking about you. People will either like you or they won't."

"Easy for you to say. Before this, my job was to be liked and unseen. Not an easy combination. And with you, I can't go unseen."

"I hope you don't want to; you are too lovely to be unseen." Apprehension washed over me and settled in the pit of my stomach. What would I do if Lia wanted to go back home? "Do you regret coming with me?"

"Of course not. I'm living a life I could have only dreamed of. It's just very different from what I thought my life would be like. It's not even that I miss my old life, I'm just still . . . adjusting to how things are now."

Relief followed the sudden feeling of panic that had come over me when I thought Lia might regret her decision to follow me to a new country. I couldn't imagine her not being here as I fumbled my way through life.

"Honoria, Lia, how wonderful it is to see you." Rika barged into the room as if she owned the place. Who was I kidding? After she married Ambrose, I wouldn't be surprised if she ended up owning half of New Lankersham. She probably thought of it as hers already.

Rika and I exchanged air kisses like they did on the Continent. Sometimes I think Rika did things just because they made her feel sophisticated, even if she didn't really understand the actions. The foreign greeting was one of those things.

"I'm surprised you have come to visit. What brings you to our hotel?" I asked.

"You haven't heard?" she asked, her eyes wide.

"No, we haven't heard anything. You know we tend to lounge a bit in the morning."

"It's all over town. They have arrested Reece Farrows for Mr. Waring's murder."

Lia gasped. "No!"

"Really? I'm surprised there was an arrest so soon. There didn't seem to be much evidence in the horse stall. More like things missing, like the racehorse Symphony, than any actual evidence left behind by the killer." My expression pensive as I gestured for everyone to take a seat.

"What? Oh, the horse! Ambrose said that Symphony was actually Mr. Waring's horse, but she had an unpleasant morning and came up lame. So, they had left the horse at home in their stables." It was not a surprise that Rika had some of the information I was looking for. She might even have files on everyone who was anyone in town.

"Oh, that at least explains one mystery, but not why they arrested Mr. Farrows so suddenly." From what I had witnessed there was nothing to tie Mr. Farrows to the crime scene.

Rika removed her gloves, indicating this would not be a short visit. "Apparently, Mr. Rochester overheard them arguing about some part of the railway before we all met up at the stables. Mr. Waring was refusing to sell, and Mr. Farrows was angry about his refusal. According to Mr. Rochester, things were very heated."

"But Mr. Farrows joined us almost as soon as we got to the races. How would Mr. Rochester have been privy to such a conversation? It doesn't make any sense. It's hard to imagine Mr. Farrows arriving at the racetrack much before us. We left the train station at about the same time. And Mr. Rochester was nowhere near the stables when we got there." I went to sit, changed my mind, and paced the sitting room. The sound of my heels emphasized my words with each step. "I want to go speak to Mr. Farrows. Something seems off about Mr. Rochester's timeline."

"Oh, Honoria, I can't imagine him lying about something like that. The man is sleeping in my home," Rika said as if one thing had to do with the other. It made sense that Mr. Rochester was staying with someone in town. The elite of society tended to host artists when they were in town. It would be considered quite the feat to host someone as prominent as Daniel Rochester.

*　　*　　*

Chapter Eight

New Lankersham, September 20, 1850

Dear Diary,

I really don't know how to explain my doubt regarding Mr. Farrows's arrest. Especially since I still think of him as a suspect. There's just something that seems off with Mr. Rochester's account of the day, but that would mean Mr. Rochester was lying, and what reason would he have to lie? I can't think of one.

It all just seems to be happening so fast; the speed of everything is wrong to me. Shouldn't the police be investigating more? How can they be so sure Mr. Farrows is the murderer?

*　　*　　*

I made my way to the jail alone. Rika had looked at me like I had lost my mind when I had mentioned it yesterday. She was more interested in the gossip than the arrest of someone she claimed was a dear friend. Lia had looked at me with a similar expression, but I knew the only way to determine what was truly happening was to speak with Mr. Farrows himself. So here I was, standing outside this unfortunate stone building, taking a deep breath to gather my composure before heading through the door.

The inside of the police station was stuffy. I don't think the building knew fall was here and the humid summer was a thing of the not-so-distant past. The doors should be left open, just to get a breeze blowing through the space. I took out my handkerchief and dabbed my brow, noting what I hoped was an information desk in front of me. I tucked the fabric into the cuff of my sleeve and approached the uniformed man with a pleasant smile pasted on my face.

Hello, sir. I was hoping you could help me out." I leaned towards the officer.

"Erm"—the officer shifted uncomfortably—"I would love to be of assistance."

"I need to speak to someone who was arrested yesterday, a Mr. Reece Farrows. Would you mind taking me to him?" I smiled at him sweetly as I clasped my hands in front of me.

"I'm not sure, Miss . . ."

"Porter."

He looked at me, waiting for me to say something more. I just stared back, eyes wide, smile in place. He blinked. I waited. He fidgeted. I waited. He looked down and grabbed a set of keys. I was secretly thrilled he had capitulated to my silence. I wanted to dance a jig in happiness, but I restrained myself. There was no need for me to gloat.

"Right this way, Miss Porter."

I followed him to the back of the building, where he unlocked a door that took us to a long hall and another locked door. The officer stepped aside. I brushed by him into a room with three barred cells. Only one of them was occupied.

"Thank you, I should be done with my conversation with Mr. Farrows in half an hour. You can come to get me then." I dismissed the officer. He stared at me, mouth agape for what felt like an interminable amount of time before nodding and leaving me alone in the cell block.

I waited a moment to ensure he did not return before I approached Mr. Farrows's cell.

"Honori . . . That is, Miss Porter. What brings you here?" he stood as if this was a normal social call, and he wasn't standing, disheveled in a jail cell.

"I came to talk to you about the murder." I looked around to see if there was something to sit or lean on, then decided I was better off standing upright.

"Right to the point: not something I expect from a lady."

I raised an eyebrow at him and saw him start to question his comment. "Yes, to the point. I don't like to mince words unless it's to my benefit. And right now, it's not. So, I'll be even more direct. Did you kill Mr. Waring to get your hands on his railroad?"

"What!" The question offended him. I could tell by the tension in his back and the furrow of his brow. "No, of course not. I would never kill someone. Much less kill someone over business."

"Assuming I believe you, why would Mr. Rochester say he overheard you arguing?"

"I really don't know. I know I didn't argue with Mr. Waring at the racetrack. However, I have argued with him in the past. But I didn't even see him at the tracks." Mr. Farrows ran his hands through his hair, somehow making it even messier.

"I heard you argue with Mr. Waring at the opera house. It wasn't a pleasant conversation. In fact, I thought you might have killed him because of the argument I overheard." I moved closer to the bars separating Mr. Farrows and me.

"And yet, you're here asking me questions. Why?" Mr. Farrows leaned against the bars.

"I don't know; maybe because you've always been a gentleman around me, even though you have information that could ruin me here in New Lankersham. Or maybe I just don't think the police did enough investigation before making an arrest. Who knows?" I paced the narrow space between the walls and the bars.

"What are you talking about?"

I stopped. "You mean you don't—"

"Remember a beautiful redhead falling out of a window into my arms?"

"Haha." I blushed and looked away. "It seems you do remember." I brushed the front of my skirts.

"Of course I remember, but I would never say anything about it. I wouldn't create trouble for someone for no reason."

"Would you say something if there was a reason?"

"If I thought it would cause harm, I would say something. But I wouldn't do it to just benefit myself, and I wouldn't say anything just to hurt someone."

"I see. Back to the day at the racetrack. Where did you go after you left the train station?"

"I just took my carriage from the station to the track. Once I was there, I went straight to the stables. I knew Ambrose would want us all there to meet Serendipity."

"Did you see anything while you were there?"

"No, I did hear about Waring's horse turning up lame, but the stall was already empty by the time I got there. Or I should say, the horse was already gone. Mr. Waring was probably already in the stall. Dead."

"Interesting and sad. He was in there for all that time." I walked to where Mr. Farrows was standing and placed my hand on his. "I should go, but I'll let you know if I learn anything."

I knocked on the door leading out of the cell block area, and the officer immediately opened it. He must have been standing there waiting for me the entire time.

"Wait, learn anything?" Mr. Farrows asked as the door closed behind the officer and me.

*   *   *

Chapter Nine

New Lankersham, September 21, 1850

Dear Diary,

There wasn't much I could do to investigate after leaving Reece in the jail cell overnight. I want to find out more, but it isn't easy to call on people I don't know all that well. I need Rika's connections to get me in. Lucky for me, Rika has sent me an invitation for afternoon tea. This will be my first chance to search for actual information.

*　　*　　*

"Are you ready, Lia?" I scurried around my room, grabbing items I thought would be useful.

"I'm not on the invitation. I don't think I should

attend." Lia sat at her vanity, pinning her curls into place.

I waved her concerns away. "Don't be silly, of course Rika is including you. She knows you are my companion, and you accompany me on all my outings. I don't understand why you believe she is always trying to exclude you."

Lia rolled her eyes. "Fine, we'll do it your way."

I waited not-so-patiently for Lia to dress for the tea. Finally ready, we left our hotel suite to take the steam-powered lift to the lobby. The walls of this amazing contraption were lined with plush velvet accented with a gilded filigree. It stopped with a hiss when it reached the lobby. The lift operator pulled the gated door open. I left our keys with the concierge and hurried to ask the doorman to hail a hansom cab for us.

It was but a moment before the doorman was escorting Lia and me into the carriage and we were on our way to Rika's. The ride was quiet. I stared out the window, watching the buildings go by. Rika lived in the most affluent part of town, while our hotel was right on the border of the fashionable part of town.

The cab came to a halt in front of a massive building. It looked more like a public building than it did a private home. Lia and I descended from the cab, taking a moment to appreciate the structure. If I were to guess, I would say the building was made of brick with a limestone facing. It was impressive, to say the least. I walked up to the carved mahogany door and used the brass knocker. The door opened to Rika's Brythionite butler. It had been explained to me that a butler from my home country was a sign of class. No one wanted a servant who didn't have the appropriate accent. I handed him my card.

"Yes, Miss Wylie Schumann is expecting you. The other guests have already arrived. They are in the parlor."

"Thank you," I said as Lia and I were escorted through the grand foyer. Inside the home was stark with all the white marble. I was used to people showing off their wealth, but New Lankersham took it to a new extreme. I wondered if it was because there was no peerage so the citizens needed to constantly prove their worth. The butler opened the doors to Rika's parlor, stepping aside so Lia and I could enter.

Inside the parlor, three ladies sat at a table set for tea with only one empty seat. I glanced back at Lia with a question in my eyes. She didn't have the same questions; instead, she gave me a knowing look.

"Hello, Rika." I walked towards my friend to greet her. I looked pointedly at the table, then back at Rika. "I thought we were invited to tea?" I stared at my friend, eyebrow raised.

Rika at least had the decency to look uncomfortable. "Honoria, I'm sorry I wasn't more specific. Let me call for another place setting."

"Really, Rika, wouldn't Miss Porter's companion be more comfortable with the other servants?" One woman at the table said. She was dripping in jewels and her clothing was made of the finest materials. I had never met her before, but it took little time to realize I didn't like her.

"I'm sorry, why would my companion be more comfortable with the servants?" I made eye contact with the woman. It wasn't long before she looked away.

"Honoria, it's fine. I really don't mind." She grabbed my shoulder, leaning in close. "Maybe I can find out something from the servants. You see what you can learn here."

I didn't want to back down from the fight in front of me, but I couldn't ignore Lia's unspoken request. I would wait to continue this when Lia wasn't around.

"If you are sure, Lia." I grabbed her hands with a squeeze. "You should be up here with me. We can leave if you would prefer."

"I know this isn't your doing. But it doesn't mean we shouldn't take advantage of the opportunity their snobbery has provided us." Lia whispered, before she turned back to the butler to be escorted to her tea elsewhere.

I made my way to the empty chair but did not sit. "I don't believe I'm acquainted with the other guests." As soon as the words left my mouth, I realized one of the women at the table was Mrs. Waring. The blatant disregard for my companion had distracted me. To the other woman, I added, "That is, I don't know you." My tone implied that I didn't care to know her. I was rude, but at this point, I wasn't overly concerned. This woman was one reason my friend was not having tea with me. I didn't much care if she liked me.

"This is Mrs. Mallory. Her husband is dear friends with Hugh Beaufort. Mr. Mallory is quite influential here in New Lankersham." Rika was still standing as if she didn't know whether to sit down for tea or have another place set, despite the fact Lia had decided for her.

As much as I didn't want to make anything easier for her, I took my seat. "How does your husband know Mr. Beaufort?"

Mrs. Waring's hand shook as she took a sip of tea. Of course, the poor thing must still be distressed about her husband's murder.

"My husband supports Mr. Beaufort's political

career. He assisted in ensuring Mr. Beaufort had the votes to win." Mrs. Mallory raised her teacup, a knowing smile on her lips.

"It must be nice having the mayor owe you a favor or two. It's not easy to win an election without a certain type of… assistance." I raised my eyebrow. This type of corruption was in the news. While Mrs. Mallory never explicitly said her husband helped cheat the system, I believed that's what she was implying.

"I never said he owed my husband anything," Mrs. Mallory spluttered. Her teacup rattled as she set it on the saucer.

"No, you didn't, but I am sure that's what you were hinting at." I turned to Mrs. Waring. "How are you? I'm happy to see you out after experiencing such a tragedy."

"I would prefer not to discuss it." She turned away from me.

"Of course." I could feel my cheeks warm; they must be turning red. "I'm so sorry."

The rest of the tea passed almost pleasantly. The sandwiches, desserts, and tea were delicious. Although, the company was lacking. Mrs. Mallory left a lot to be desired in an afternoon companion. I had never listened to someone describe the ways in which they had money and power quite so thoroughly. At home, it would have been considered extremely gauche and not tolerated.

Tea ended. Normally, I would think it ended too soon. This one had lasted forever. The four of us stood to say our goodbyes. For the first time, I noticed just how tall Mrs. Waring was. She towered over me, which said very little, but she was also taller than Rika and Mrs. Mallory.

*   *   *

Chapter Ten

New Lankersham, September 21, 1850

Dear Diary,

I have never been so embarrassed and appalled in my life. Even though my mother is, well, my mother. I hoped this country would be different; it was supposed to be different. Instead, someone I thought was my friend had made someone who is actually my friend feel like she wasn't worthy of having tea with the rest of us. I'm going to fix this. This is the last time someone treats a person important to me that way.

*   *   *

I closed the door to our hotel suite, leaning against

the door as it clicked shut.

"Lia, I'm so sorry. You kept telling me Rika was— snobbish, but I refused to listen. I'm so sorry. I won't let this happen again. And I'll talk to Rika about it this afternoon or, maybe, tomorrow."

"It's fine, it's the way of the world." Lia was ever pragmatic.

I pushed myself off the door. "It's not the way of my world. So, I will have a word with Rika."

"If you think it will make a difference, you can try. Maybe it will help. I have more interesting things to talk about, though." Lia leaned forward on the settee.

"Oh really? What did you learn?" I sat next to her, ready to temporarily forget the behavior of this afternoon.

Lia smirked. "It turns out our grieving widow might not actually be grieving. Apparently, she's been having an affair with Mr. Beaufort for quite a while now."

"No!" I gasped. Mrs. Waring had seemed so submissive on the few occasions we met. I couldn't see her having the gumption it took to have an affair.

"Yes, it was the talk of the servants. The real gossip was whether or not Mr. Waring had found out. If he had, the chef said Mr. Waring would not have let her survive. The mayor and Mrs. Waring were discreet. The Mallorys didn't even know about the affair, and they apparently know everything that happens in town. They are quite the powerful couple."

I drummed my fingers on the back of the settee, thinking back to some of the conversations during tea. "That does coincide with her reaction every time someone mentioned Hugh Beaufort."

"What do you mean?"

"Mrs. Waring seemed more nervous every time his name was mentioned. One time, her hands shook so much her teacup chattered on the saucer. I wonder if Mr. Waring knew about the affair. If he did, really even if he didn't, Mrs. Waring has a motive to want Mr. Waring gone." I stood, moving about the room as I thought.

"It would also give Mr. Beaufort a motive as well. Especially if Mr. Waring was preventing them from being together."

"True, Mr. Beaufort had something else going on. Something having to do with his election and becoming the mayor. Mrs. Mallory hinted at what sounded like corruption. But it would only have to do with the murder if Mr. Waring knew about it. It makes me wonder exactly what Mr. Waring knew."

"Here's something else that Mr. Waring knew. I was

told by Rika's servants that Ambrose was being blackmailed by Mr. Waring. He said Ambrose was adding something to the horse's grain to either slow down a competitor's horse or speed up his. They said the reason Symphony didn't race was because Ambrose or his men got to her."

I had stopped pacing when Lia mentioned the horses' feed. "I can't believe that Ambrose would harm a horse. Did you see him around Serendipity? That man loves animals."

Lia shrugged. "It's the gossip going around the servants' quarters. I'm not sure it's true."

"If Mr. Waring threatened to say something about it, Ambrose might have had a motive, even if the rumors are false. It could destroy his reputation before he could prove that he wasn't doing anything wrong."

"The question is where does that leave the investigation?" Lia asked.

"It means we have more than just suspects. Now, we have motives as well. I think I should make some calls. I'd also love to know if Mr. Waring knew anything about anyone else who's a suspect." I looked knowingly at Lia. It was time we intentionally split up. Lia could talk to the Warings' servants, and I could make my way through some of the other suspects.

"Who are you planning to call on?" Lia looked at me,

suspicion in her tone.

"I think I'll start with Rika and Ambrose. At the very least, I can see if I can clear Ambrose of any wrongdoing. Maybe I'll try to talk to the jockey as well. If Ambrose was up to anything, he would know." I paused. My other reason for starting there was that I owed Rika a taste of my anger. I didn't want Lia to know, but I was still seething on the inside. "And I think I want to speak to Mr. Farrows again. I wonder if he knows more than he's letting on. Then there's Mr. Beaufort and Mrs. Waring; someone needs to speak to the people who know the most about them." I glanced over at Lia. She rolled her eyes.

"Of course, I'll talk to the servants at each of their houses. Find out enough about them that I can start my own gossip column. New Lankersham society has as much to hide as the *ton* did in Fintan." Lia smiled wickedly.

"So it would seem. Only this time, no one is trying to hide any information about me. I wonder how my mother is faring now that I'm gone. I bet she's happy only having my sister, the biddable Olivia, left at home." My skirts billowed as I sat down suddenly.

"You know you can always write them. Let her know where you are and that you are safe."

"If I did that, they would send someone to take me

back home. No, it's better they don't know where I am or what I'm doing. At least not until I've been gone for so long that there's no need to send someone after me." I stared out the window, looking out over a city that was nothing like home, as memories of the place I ran from flitted through my head.

*   *   *

Chapter Eleven

New Lankersham, September 22, 1850

Dear Diary,

To say I'm perplexed by the information Lia has discovered is the understatement of the year. Ambrose seems too jovial to do anything dastardly. In fact, if you were to ask me who in the relationship between Ambrose and Rika is more likely to murder someone, I would say it is Rika. She seems the type that would do anything to reach her goals, and I do mean anything. Sometimes I wonder if I'm like that as well, but I do believe there are lines that should not be crossed.

*   *   *

After a productive breakfast with Lia where we each laid out our plans for the day, I made my way to Rika's home. It was too early for a proper call, but I wasn't going there to socialize. I needed to say some things, and my friend needed to sit and hear them, whether or not she liked it. With those thoughts in my head, I strode with a purpose down the cobblestone sidewalks of New Lankersham, my heels tapping out the staccato rhythm of someone on a mission.

It seemed like mere moments had passed as I stood in front of the imposing door to Rika's home. I took a deep breath and knocked, brushing my hands down the grey wool of my dress while I waited for the butler to open the door. The creak of the door drew my eyes up from the ground as the door was opened just enough to turn me away. However, that did not coincide with my plans today. I pushed the door wide open and stepped into the massive foyer.

"Can you please let Miss Wylie Schumann know I am here to see her?" I strode into the parlor. "I will wait in the parlor. Please have a tea tray sent in."

The butler attempted to not look flabbergasted as I ordered him to do my bidding.

"Yes, I will see to it." He turned with a sharp nod and left the room.

It was but a moments before tea arrived. The frenzied

maid set it out before me, allowing me to get a whiff of orange and warm spices.

"Thank you, this smells absolutely delightful," I said with a smile.

The maid looked at me, eyes wide, like she wasn't sure how I was able to see her. She nodded at me before scurrying out of the room.

I sat there enjoying the warmth of the tea and the little apple cakes that had been brought out with it. The cozy flavors helped to ward off the chill of the cold and uninviting room.

"Honoria, whatever has brought you here so early in the day?" Rika burst through the massive double doors that led into the room. She looked resplendent in her purple velvet dressing gown. I was amazed someone could look that good and not be dressed for company.

"There are a few things I need to discuss with you, and unfortunately, it could not wait until later, when other guests could be visiting." I could hear the edge in my tone.

"Oh, do tell. Have you learned something salacious?" Rika sat in the chair across from me and leaned forward.

"Potentially, if any of it is true, which is one of the reasons that I'm here. But first, I have something to say that I don't think you are going to like very much. Yesterday—

excluding Lia from the tea—it was truly unacceptable. Lia told me she didn't think you liked her very much or that you wanted her at any of the events that you have invited me to, but I dismissed how she felt as being overly sensitive. Yesterday, I was embarrassed and saddened to discover I was wrong." I stood and paced the length of the carpet in the room. It was beautiful with all of its vibrant colors. I wondered if it was Latikan? I shook the thought out of my head. I needed to stay on task.

"Honoria, dear, I don't see why it's such a bother. Lia was happy down with the other servants."

"Lia is not a servant, Rika. She's my companion and dear friend. She should be treated as such." I stopped pacing and stood there, hands on my hips. The only thing missing from my speech was an emphatic foot stomp.

"A companion is a servant, aren't they? I wouldn't want Lia to feel uncomfortable dining with her . . ." Rika stopped speaking when I held up my hand.

"Her what? Betters?" I laughed. "I feel you are not understanding me. Maybe back in Brythion, Lia would have been relegated to the downstairs. However, we are not in Brythion. We are here, in Eletharis, the land of equality and opportunity. It seems you and your friends have forgotten that. If I am to continue this friendship, you must know it comes with Lia not as a servant but as an equal. Just like I treat you as an equal, even though I'm the daughter of a lord and your family is in trade."

"How dare . . ." Rika's face heated.

My tone softened. "Take a moment to feel what you are feeling, and then think of Lia here yesterday afternoon, coming into the room, being dismissed by Mrs. Mallory as beneath her, and discovering you didn't even put a place setting out for her."

I watched as emotions played across Rika's face. She flushed with anger, then reddened with what I could only hope was embarrassment.

"Oh dear, you're correct, Honoria." Rika took in a deep breath. "That was not well done of me, and I will not let it happen again."

I sat in the chair next to Rika. "That's that then. Let's move on to the more salacious topics." I leaned forward. "Did you know that Mrs. Waring and Mr. Beaufort were having an affair?"

"Oh my, they were? I never heard anything about the two of them even interacting with each other. Not a single rumor that connected them. That being said, I can see how Mrs. Waring would want to seek companionship with someone else. Mr. Waring was a tough character, obsessed with his little railway and the power it gave him, obsessed with power in general."

"Really? I'd heard him argue about the railway, but I didn't realize he was seeking political power."

"Oh yes, he tried to get Ambrose to support him in some business or another. It was basically blackmail. He accused Ambrose of drugging horses, said he would keep it secret if we supported his run for mayor next election," Rika said.

"So, you've heard the rumors about Ambrose drugging his horses? Last night I heard the rumor for the first time. Anyone who has seen Ambrose with his horses would know in an instant he would never engage in behavior that could harm them," I said. "I was worried for you and Ambrose that if those rumors got out, it would harm Ambrose even if they weren't true."

"It would be terrible if the rumors got out. It's why Ambrose told Mr. Waring he would think about supporting him in the next election. He stopped bothering us for a bit. But at the race, he approached Ambrose again. He even threatened to say he wasn't racing his horse because Ambrose drugged it. The man had a plan and was ruthless in how he went about executing it." Rika's hands shook as she spoke.

"It's convenient that he is dead. Solves the problem Ambrose was having with him," I muttered under my breath, not that I believed Ambrose was capable of such an act, even if he did have a valid motive.

"You can't possibly think Ambrose would kill anyone? We would have found some way to protect his reputation in the racing circles." Rika stared, taking in every emotion that ran across my face. "You do think he could have done this horrible thing: it's all over your face." Rika stood, ready to have me escorted out.

"That isn't it, Rika. I'm here because I want to confirm my belief that Ambrose is innocent. I can't see him hurting anyone or anything. Mr. Farrows is innocent too, at least I believe he is." I grabbed Rika's hands. "I need to ensure none of my dear friends are blamed for a crime they didn't commit. So, you see, I need to know more about anyone who could be involved, however unlikely the person is to be a killer. It's the only reason I would ask about Ambrose at all."

*　　*　　*

Chapter Twelve

New Lankersham, September 22, 1850

Dear Diary,

It was such a relief to get the necessary chat with
Rika out of the way and to tell her what I had heard about
Ambrose. I really feel like we understand each other better
now. At least that is my hope. To that end, I let Rika convince
me to go talk to Mr. And Mrs. Mallory. She thinks it would
be a good way to find out more about Hugh Beaufort. I have
to agree, especially because he seems super suspicious to
me. He definitely has a lot to hide.

*   *   *

"I have a fantastic idea, Honoria." Rika placed her tea

down on the tray I had ordered. "We should call on Mrs. Mallory now. If we're lucky, Mr. Mallory will still be there. We could find out more about the mayor."

I looked at Rika; she was on the edge of her seat waiting for me to respond. I wanted to continue to investigate, but I wasn't sure about including Rika. However, she could get me into places that I couldn't get into on my own. It just felt too early to dismiss Ambrose as a suspect completely, and I didn't want Rika to be around for that part of the investigation. I needed to talk to people in the horse racing world on my own, but it wouldn't hurt to talk to Rika's friends first.

"That's a great idea. I would love your help," I said.

Rika stood with a clap of her hands. "This will be so fun. Give me a moment to change."

"Of course. I will wait here for you." I watched as Rika practically ran out of the room, leaving me alone with my cup of tea and swirling thoughts. I wanted to know who killed Mr. Waring, but it felt like I had to find out something else first, like I needed to know more about Mr. Waring to know who murdered him. In this investigation, it seemed like the why would lead me to the who, so I had assumed the who would lead me to the why. But right now, that felt wrong.

Three lemon blueberry tarts, two cucumber sandwiches, and one cup of tea later, Rika was ready to go. I insisted we could walk, but she called for a carriage anyway. She was appalled that I would suggest walking three blocks and flabbergasted when I told her I thought getting a horse and carriage out for three blocks was a complete waste of time. She insisted the Mallorys would find it amiss if we showed up at their door on foot, so I gave in. Who was I to say what her friends would or would not think? It caused me to long for my dear friends back home. I missed how Brythionites insisted on showing status. It was more understated and definitely less flashy, unless, of course, one was new money.

I shook my head and any lingering thoughts away. It was time to focus on what Mrs. Mallory might know and how to get her to speak of it.

"Do you have any idea how involved Mrs. Mallory is in politics or anything else that might get us information?" I asked my friend as the carriage began it's three block journey.

Rika leaned towards me conspiratorially. "I'm not sure, but she has often bragged about how her husband made sure Beaufort was elected. It makes me think she knows quite a bit. In fact, I would hazard a guess that she's the mastermind of it all, and her husband is just the purse strings."

The carriage came to a halt in front of yet another massive brick building. Rika and I alighted from our seats and made our way to the door. Rika grabbed the impressive-looking knocker and banged it three times. Another stuffy butler answered the door.

"Yes?" he asked, raising an imperious eyebrow.

"Good day, please let Mrs. Mallory know Miss Wylie Schumann and Miss Porter are here to see her." She held out her calling card to the elderly man.

"I will have to see if Mrs. Mallory is home." The butler took the card, seemingly against his will, posture stiff with his own importance.

"You and I both know she is home. We will wait inside while you fetch her," Rika said.

Apparently, I was not the only one who was willing to steamroll a servant to get something done, which led to the two of us standing in the foyer waiting for Mrs. Mallory to decide whether or not to see us.

"Rika, darling, how lovely to see you—and your little friend, Miss Poncer, I do believe." Mrs. Mallory swept into the room with all the aplomb of a melodramatic stage performer.

"It's Miss Porter," I said with clipped tones.

"Ah, yes, that's right." She nodded in agreement as if it was her decision as to what my name was. She turned to Rika. "What brings you here at this time of day?"

"I was just dying for a bit of gossip," Rika said in a hushed tone. "I just recently heard the most interesting things about Hugh Beaufort, and with the murder and everything else, I was wondering if anyone knew whether or not the rumors were true?"

"It would be quite nice if we could sit somewhere," I said. "I don't think this is a conversation to be had in the foyer." I nodded toward the butler.

"Of course. Let's all have a seat in the morning room." Mrs. Mallory led us down the foyer hall to a door on the left. She opened the door with a flourish. "Here we are."

I stood there, speechless. I knew Junhar art was quite popular now, but a room full of antiquities of another culture was a bit much. That didn't stop me from perusing; after all, my goal was to eventually visit these countries and explore an archaeological dig. This would do for now, though.

"You have quite the collection," I said, stopping in front of an intricately designed side table.

"My husband is very generous. He's found so many pieces for my collection. After all, Junhar art is all the rage right now."

"The historical and cultural significance of these pieces is impressive. They look like they belong in a museum." I didn't even try to hide the disapproval that laced my words.

"I've never really cared about any of that. I just enjoy having the pieces here." Mrs. Mallory gestured for me to sit.

"I see." And I really did see her reasons, even if I didn't agree with them. I sat on a settee inspired by Junhar hieroglyphs. There were gold images woven into the green tapestry, and the wood was carved into a stylistic pattern and painted a shiny black. Some might think it was beautiful, but I thought it was tacky.

"What do you want to know about Hugh Beaufort? Or better yet, what have you heard?" Mrs. Mallory asked Rika.

Rika leaned forward conspiratorially. "I just recently heard that Mr. Beaufort and Mrs. Waring were having an affair. I can barely believe it. Until now, I'd heard nothing about it. I also heard that he stole the mayoral election. Either he or someone backing him hired men to stuff the ballot boxes, voting multiple times."

Mrs. Mallory turned an unbecoming shade of red, picked at the pleats in her skirt, and shifted in her seat.

"I'm surprised ballot stuffing works. Doesn't the city keep track of the population, and couldn't they compare the number of votes to the eligible voting population in the city? It would stop corruption in the elections here," I said, ignoring the fact that Mrs. Mallory looked apoplectic.

Mrs. Mallory took a deep breath. "Corruption? I wouldn't call it that. Just politics."

"Are you saying it's true?" Rika asked. She sounded disappointed.

"It's corrupt because Mr. Beaufort is controlled by whoever put him in office. They can hold it over his head his entire term." I stood, my body wanting to move, but I remembered this was not my home, so I sat back down. "I wonder if anyone knew about the fixed election?"

"Fixed. All these words you're using make it sound so bad." Mrs. Mallory let out a high-pitched laugh.

"What else would you call it?" I asked.

"Helping the city elect the best candidate for the job."

"But it's the opinion of whoever is fixing the race, not the entire city. What makes them think they are right?"

"That's exactly what Mr. Waring said when he confronted my husband and Mr. Beaufort. Mr. Waring was trying to convince us to support him and for Hugh to step down. When my husband wouldn't do it, Mr. Waring took

Mr. Beaufort aside. Their conversation looked heated, but I wasn't able to hear anything that was said. But you could tell they did not leave on friendly terms."

"It sounds like Mr. Waring was up to something, something other than running for mayor," I murmured, deep in thought.

*   *   *

Chapter Thirteen

New Lankersham, September 23, 1850

Dear Diary,

I really need to speak to the mayor, and I'm not quite sure how to make that happen. It's not like I could just walk up to Mr. Beaufort and ask, did you kill Mr. Waring? I am more convinced than ever that I need to talk to Mr. Farrows. I think he knows more than he's telling me. How am I supposed to help him if he's not open about everything? At least talking to him is easy, easier than cornering the mayor, at least for now.

*   *   *

I stared at the offensive pile of clothes on my bed, not

satisfied that any of the ensembles would set the right tone for the day. They all seemed so frivolous. I sighed.

"What's going on in there?" Lia asked from the hall.

I swung open the door and gestured to the mountain of fabric on my bed. "I have nothing to wear today."

Lia walked into the room, pausing when she saw the mound of clothes enveloping my bed. "I fear that's never going to be an actual problem for you. Clearly, there's a mound of clothing on your bed you could be wearing."

"None of them are right." I grabbed my mint-green dressing gown and threw it over my undergarments.

"What are you trying to accomplish?"

"I want to get in to see the mayor and Mr. Farrows. I know I can see Mr. Farrows, but Mr. Beaufort isn't stuck behind bars. Makes it a little more difficult to force my presence on him."

"I see. Why don't you just talk to Mr. Beaufort at Rika's party in a few nights? She's invited us over; she actually included me on the invite this time for a musical at her house. Apparently, she finally convinced Daniel Rochester to play for her guests." Lia explained as she went through my garments, creating a few different piles.

"What? I didn't think he ever played for private audiences any longer. I've never understood why. He is a guest in her home while he's performing in town. One would think he could afford to stay at a hotel instead of for free at a private residence. And if he is staying at a private residence, there should be some type of exchange, like a private night of music," I rambled. "I'm sorry. I don't know why I'm so easily distracted today."

"You don't like to feel stuck, and I if I were to guess, you are out of sorts because you don't think you know enough about this investigation you decided to take on."

"You're right. But I have to do something. I can't let an innocent man be punished for a crime he didn't commit." I sat at my vanity and stared blankly at myself.

"Here, this is what you should wear to see Mr. Farrows," Lia said, tossing the ensemble towards me.

I lost sight of myself in the mirror as the dress Lia chose engulfed me. She must have picked out one of my ruffled skirts because it felt like I pushed miles of fabric out of the way before I saw daylight and Lia's smirking face again. I guess my bout of melancholy was not to be tolerated today. I felt a smile tug at the corner of my lips as I assessed myself in the mirror, head barely peeking out of a swath of green-and-bronze-striped silk. Unable to hold back anymore, I burst out laughing.

"How was your trip to the Waring's home? Did the

servants open up to you?" I asked as I bent over to put on my boots.

"I thought you would never ask." Lia sat down on my bed, piles of clothes surrounding her. She leaned forward. "The Warings' servants were all too happy to talk to me, definitely lacking in loyalty, but Mr. Waring didn't seem to inspire any dedication at all. And if there was a reason to stay quiet, it's gone now that he's dead."

"Was he abusive? Did he not pay well?" I asked.

"Apparently, he didn't pay well, but that changed a few months ago. Some of the servants even thought he had inherited a large sum recently. He had gone from being miserly to borderline generous." Lia fidgeted with the hem of one of my skirts.

"Fascinating. I wonder what changed," I said with a raised eyebrow.

"From what I can tell, he got a toehold in higher society circles."

Standing, I took the clothes Lia had tossed onto my head with me behind my dressing screen. I hung up the bodice, followed by my dressing gown leaving me in my corset, petticoat, and pantaloons. Then I started the process of putting on the many layers of women's clothing. Before I reached for my crinoline, I pulled my corset cover on.

"That's interesting. I would think he would have less money to go around, not more."

"Unless he was using his access to the people in his new social circles to get money."

"You mean blackmail?" My voice was muffled as I attempted to shimmy my way into the fifth layer of skirt material. The number of petticoats required to maintain the shape of today's fashion was ridiculous. At least the green-and-bronze stripes looked good together, and the ruffles helped create the appropriate shape. Thankfully, the silk of the skirt was lightweight, so I could still walk even with the weight of three petticoats, a crinoline, and an overskirt buttoned around my waist.

"I don't know what else it could be, and it would give someone, potentially a few someones, a motive for murder."

I stuck my head out from behind the screen. "How am I going to talk to someone who knows about the blackmail, or better yet, someone who was one of Mr. Waring's victims?" I grabbed my bodice and button hook. The tool was brilliant: it made buttoning up a bodice three times faster. In just a few moments, I was dressed and ready for the day.

"I wonder if he tried to blackmail Mr. Farrows. He's already in jail for the crime. It shouldn't be hard to talk to him."

"At least he'll be a captive audience."

* * *

Chapter Fourteen

New Lankersham, September 23, 1850

Dear Diary,

Seeing Mr. Farrows reminded me of just how handsome he is. I really hope he isn't a murderer. I would hate to be so wrong about someone's character. It would also be a shame to waste such a face on a killer. All I can really say is I don't think the trip to the jail was a complete waste.

*   *   *

"I'm here to see Mr. Farrows," I announced to the bobby at the desk. It was my goal to strike a tone somewhere between authoritarian and ladylike. Too much of either and I was likely to be turned away.

"Are you sure, Miss . . ." The young officer paused, and I realized he didn't know my name.

"Porter. And of course, I'm sure. Why would I ask to see him if I wasn't sure?" I placed my hands on the desk and leaned forward.

"But the person you requested to see is being held for murder. I don't think I should let a lady like you speak to him." His eyes darted around the room, searching for someone else to pawn me off on.

"Yes, I know what Mr. Farrows has been accused of. That's why I am here. I do not believe in his guilt. Now, please, can you show me to his cell?" I stood as tall as my petite form would allow.

The young officer rubbed the back of his neck and looked around the room for backup, but all the other men in the room were either busy or purposefully ignoring them. It was almost enough to make me laugh. Instead, I strode towards the cells, leaving him no choice but to follow me. I heard keys jangle and assumed he had given in to my request.

"Don't you need a chaperone or something, Miss?" he asked as he pushed the key into the keyhole, pausing before opening the door.

"He's behind bars. I don't think he's a risk to my virtue. However, if it makes you feel better, I promise I'll stay out of his reach. I managed to do just that the last time we spoke."

He turned the key and opened the door. I brushed past him into the holding cell area. The only occupant of the room prior to my entering was Mr. Farrows. He sat on a narrow cot with his back resting up against the stone wall and his arm propped up on one leg. The other leg hung off the edge of the small bed; his fingers continuously thrummed on his thigh. He was in quite a state of disarray—his head was covered only by his tousled hair, his coat off, his cravat untied, the top two buttons of his shirt undone. I looked back at the young officer, indicating that he should close the door. He looked as if he was going to protest again, so I raised an eyebrow. With a sigh, he closed the door, leaving Mr. Farrows and me alone.

I turned back to Mr. Farrows. "I see you were not expecting any company. Are there no local debutantes coming around to soothe your forlorn soul?"

"Alas, no. Only you, Miss Porter, have demeaned yourself and come to see this accused murderer." He opened his eyes and stared at me.

I shivered; most of the men I was acquainted with never took the time to see me. They saw only what they wanted to see, which always aligned with where I fit into their world. For some reason, when Reece looked at me like he was now, I felt seen. I took a step forward but stopped myself before taking another step.

"I don't see a murderer in front of me, but a man

wrongly accused," I said. "I'm also certain that you are keeping something from me. And how am I supposed to solve this so you can be released from jail if you aren't open with me about everything?"

"Who said that I expected you to solve anything? It isn't safe for you to be investigating a murder. The killer could come after you. Have you even considered that possibility?"

I couldn't help but roll my eyes at his condescension. "Of course, I've assessed the dangers. I am a woman: I am constantly aware of what dangers could lurk around every corner and behind every door. If I lived my life only thinking of what bad things could happen, I wouldn't be living a life. So why don't you tell me more about your interactions with Mr. Waring?"

"You already know he didn't want to sell the railway he owned. What more do you want to know?" Reece stood and walked over to the bars and casually leaned against them.

"What I want to know is—did he try to blackmail you? And if he did, why?" I drifted closer to where Reece was leaning.

"How do you know about the blackmail—well, attempted blackmail?"

"I have my ways." So much for keeping my distance. "What do you mean, attempted blackmail?"

"Mr. Waring tried to blackmail me, but he had nothing to threaten me with. So it didn't work."

I leaned in farther, fascinated that Mr. Waring, someone who was thought of as a gentleman, was so nefarious. "What did he want from you?"

"Political backing. If he had just asked, I might have considered it. Beaufort's an idiot controlled by the Mallorys. But he started with threats: instead of trying to establish a rapport, he said he would tell everyone of the cuts I had made, ignoring the safety of my employees and passengers. He even claimed someone had died due to my negligence. Except none of that had ever happened. I would never risk the life of another like that. Especially not for money."

"What did he do when you refused? Rumors like that could ruin you, even if they weren't true."

The two of us leaned towards each other, intently focused on every word the other said. Or maybe it was just me focusing on the way his mouth moved and the fullness of his lips.

"I was ready to combat the rumors, legally. I sat for interviews with a few local papers and discussed the importance of safety and the lives of those who work for me.

How I would not have a railroad at all if it weren't for the risks they were willing to take on a day-to-day basis. Because of their commitment to me and my company, I felt it was necessary to commit to providing them with the safest workplace I possibly could, so I would never cut corners to save a few pennies. Those articles were published before he could act on his threats. It didn't stop him from trying something new though. He came around accusing me of doping my racehorse. I ignored that accusation since I wasn't planning on running any more races. He seemed quite desperate."

Reece lowered his head ever so slightly.

"He used the same horse-doping threat on Ambrose. It seemed he was recycling ideas. He was also terrible at researching his targets. Why would he think his threats would work if the individuals he was threatening hadn't done anything wrong?" I pondered.

"Reputation is everything in society. Truth is next to meaningless."

"It was like that back in Brythion as well. But would anyone kill to stop the spread of a false rumor? That seems highly unlikely. I wonder if Mr. Waring did find out some unsavory truths about someone. Maybe Mr. Beaufort or even Daniel Rochester."

"Funny you should mention Daniel Rochester. I saw them arguing after the symphony. I don't know what it was about, but it looked quite heated."

"I'm surprised they knew each other. Mr. Rochester has agreed to play at a soirée Rika is having in a few nights."

"What I wouldn't give to see that; he never plays at house parties."

"Maybe I'll have you out by then." I tilted my head back just a bit.

After that statement, our lips met. I'm not sure how it happened, but the gentle pressure turned into something more intense. His hands found my waist and pulled me up against the bars. A loud clang brought me back to the moment, and I jumped away.

"I've wanted to do that since you fell into my arms," Reece said as I all but ran to the station door.

*   *   *

Chapter Fifteen

New Lankersham, September 24, 1850

Dear Diary,

What a kiss! I can't believe that happened, or maybe I can. It seems I have a weakness for a handsome face. Reece kissed better than anyone else I have ever kissed. I wouldn't mind kissing him again, but it wouldn't do at all to go around kissing murderers. Which means I need to find another suspect. Today, I intend to drag Lia with me to the racetrack. Hopefully, we can find the jockey and ask him about the horse-doping scandal and maybe learn something else Mr. Waring could have blackmailed someone about. Everyone has something to hide. The question is, did Mr.

Waring ever find a person to give him what he wanted?

*   *   *

"Lia, are you ready to go? We can still make the early train if we hurry." I heard shuffling and then a bang, causing me to wince. Lia was not great in the mornings. Instead of waking her to get help to dress, I'd made changes to my wardrobe to be able to dress myself, which had allowed Lia to sleep later and later.

Lia ran into the room, skidding to a halt in front of me.

"I'm sorry, Honoria," she panted. "Comfortable beds will be my downfall. It makes sleeping so much more fun."

I couldn't help but laugh at her statement. "It's the beds? Not your general disdain for mornings?"

"That might play into it, but it's mostly the beds. The bed I had as a servant was not nearly as welcoming as anything I've slept on since taking off on this journey with you." Lia smiled lost in thoughts of comfortable sleeping arrangements.

I winced at the thought of all my parents' servants sleeping on uncomfortable beds. "That's unfortunate. Everyone should be able to get a good night's sleep. I'm happy to hear you haven't come to regret my escapades yet. Now, let's go. We can still make the first train if we hurry."

Lia haphazardly jabbed the hatpin into her hat and threw on her cloak. She then looked at me as if she'd been waiting for me all morning and not the other way around. I burst out laughing as I walked past her. My mother would have talked to the housekeeper, and Lia would have been scolded for her impertinence. I, on the other hand, loved it. Maybe my leaving was more than the whim of a little rich girl. I might just be doing some good in the world.

A brisk walk to the station and a mad dash to the platform allowed Lia and me to board the train with a modicum of decorum. Mr. Farrows really knew how to make travel comfortable, or as comfortable as possible. I was, once again, in awe of how luxurious the train car was as it made its way to Sandison Downs. The rhythmic chug of the train and the constantly moving scenery matched my continually wandering thoughts. It seemed with each chug I was thinking of something new, unable to focus on one thought for long, just like I couldn't focus on any view for more than a minute.

The sound of the train slowed down until it halted at the station. I nudged Lia, hoping she was awake enough to follow me out, before grabbing my things and exiting the train. Once Lia and I had disembarked, I scanned the road for a hansom cab, one with a driver who looked particularly honest. It always amazed me how often men said they wanted to protect a lady but were always the first to try to take advantage of us.

"That one I think." I pointed, looking up to see if Lia agreed.

"He looks like my grandfather. Hopefully, that means he's nice, like my grandfather." Lia made her way through the crowd towards an elderly driver with a full white beard and blue-wool cap.

I followed a step behind her. A constant debate of ours was who cleared a path quicker and why: did she clear one because of her height and angelic beauty, or did I because of my fiery red hair and purposeful stride? Clearly, her height won out because everyone stepped aside as she moved through the station. I got more annoyed glances than people moving out of my way the majority of the time.

"Good morning, or should I say afternoon, Mister . . .," Lia started.

"Shade, it's Mr. Shade," the driver answered.

"I was hoping you could take us to the racetracks; we have some business to take care of there."

"What business would a lady have at a racetrack?" the man asked.

"The same as any man, I would assume. My lady here is the proud new owner of a racehorse and needs to talk to the jockey she hired before the next race," Lia responded, perfectly poised.

"If you say so. Might as well take you; there aren't many fares coming off the train today," he grumbled.

"Perfect," Lia said, nodding for me to get into the cab before she followed me in.

It was a bone-jarring, quick-paced ride to the track. I had to hold on just to stay in my seat as it felt like the driver's goal was to take every corner on two wheels. By the time the cab stopped, I all but tumbled out. Anything to not be in that box anymore. I brushed my skirts down and took a deep breath as Lia also rushed to disembark.

Pasting a smile on my face, I thanked the man and threw him the coin that covered the trip.

"Let's go find Mr. MacGregor and hope that we can forget about that ride," I said.

"It was rather something, wasn't it?"

The two of us walked in silence to the stables. I was, yet again, impressed with Lia and her intuitiveness. She seemed to read my moods better than any of my other friends. She laughed with me when that was what I needed and walked with me when my mood insisted on silence.

"Is that him, Honoria?" Lia asked, interrupting my reverie. She pointed to a short and skinny man walking a beautiful black horse.

"I do believe it is," I responded. "Mr. MacGregor!" I called out and waved when the young man turned.

He stopped and waited as Lia and I approached, a questioning look on his face.

"Yes, miss?" he asked as I stopped in front of him.

"I was hoping you could spare a moment; I have heard some rumors around town about horse doping, and I was wondering if you could enlighten me on the subject."

"Well, miss, I don't know I have much to say about it." He shuffled his feet and refused to look me in the eye.

"I'm not here to get you in trouble. All I want is to learn all I can about Mr. Waring so I can help my friend that has been accused of his murder. I don't believe he did it, and I know Mr. Waring accused some people of this act, including Mr. Jacobs." I felt like I was babbling, but I wanted to walk that fine line between ladylike and overly competent. Babbling always seemed to put men at ease, like it was a quality they expected me to have, and now that I had it, they could easily determine where I fit in their world.

"I . . . That is . . . There are some people here that have participated in doping, but Mr. Jacobs would never do such a thing. Mr. Waring tried to get me to do it behind Mr. Jacobs's back and was quite mad when I refused. I was relieved when that music gentleman interrupted us."

"Mr. Rochester?" Lia asked.

The horse jockey seemed to notice Lia for the first time. His eyes widened and his jaw became slack.

"I . . . Well . . . I . . . don't think I can say, but he . . . he's been performing in town."

"Did you happen to overhear anything that the man had to say?" I asked, briefly tearing the man's attention away from Lia. I almost laughed at Mr. MacGregor's instant infatuation with my companion.

"I think he said something about not letting Mr. Waring ruin his life, but I didn't really stop to listen."

I made eye contact with Lia. This was an unexpected development.

*　　*　　*

Chapter Sixteen

New Lankersham, September 25, 1850

Dear Diary,

With all the information I have gathered recently, I feel like I know who the killer is, but I don't know why. Actually, if I'm honest with myself, I think the killer could be one of two people, but I'm leaning towards one more than the other. I just need to find some actual evidence to back up one of my theories. Right now, one of my suspects had a clear motive while the other had the opportunity. Who knows, maybe they formed some sort of alliance and were both in on it. The important thing is, I do believe I have enough to convince the police to release Mr. Farrows.

*   *   *

"I'm off to see if I can speak with the mayor. I think I can convince him to release Mr. Farrows based on what I've learned. What are you doing today?" My voice was muffled as I shimmied an emerald silk ruffled skirt over my head and down to my waist.

Lia yawned, stretching as she did so. "Nothing until we head to Rika's for lunch."

"Perfect. I should be back by then. We can go together. I want to snoop if I can."

"Honoria, you always want to snoop." Lia lay back on the pillows on my bed. I was certain to find her there after taking care of my morning business.

"I'll see you when I get back," I said as I jabbed my hat pin through my hat.

Lia sighed with contentment as she burrowed farther into the bed. "Mmmmhmmm."

I laughed as I left my room. Lia living her best life was an amazing side benefit of my escape from Brython. I stepped into the steam-powered elevator, closed the gate with a click, and listened to the machinery work as it lowered me to the ground level of the hotel. I pushed the gate open and stepped out of the elevator, my heeled boots striking the marble floor in a crisp rhythm as I walked across the lobby. The uniformed doorman opened the door as I approached and nodded hello like he did every morning as I left. The pattern was comforting, even though it was getting boring.

Walking through the city was always interesting. So many men rushed off to different jobs. There were women off to work as well, but not nearly as many and most of them were servants. There was so much hustle and bustle it made me walk even faster to my destination. It wasn't long before I was standing in front of the capitol building,

I took a deep breath before walking up all the steps and through the doors.

"Can I help you, miss?" a young man behind a heavy wood desk asked.

"Yes, I need to speak to Mayor Beaufort." I looked at the man with unwavering steadiness. Sometimes it seemed like if you acted like you belonged, others believed it was true. So, that was how I acted most of the time.

"Of course. Do you have an appointment?"

"I'm supposed to. My secretary came by last week to schedule one," I lied with a concerned look on my face. "It would be under Miss Honoria Porter."

"Ah, yes, here you are."

There was no way I was on that list.

"If you wait here, I'll let the mayor know you are here."

I wasn't going to wait and give Mr. Beaufort the opportunity to not see me.

"Thank you. I will follow you to his office."

"I think it's best if you stay and wait."

"That may be best for you, but for me, I would rather just follow you. I don't have long and would love to finish with this business quickly." It was a weak explanation, but an explanation nonetheless.

"Mayor, there's a Miss . . ."

"Mayor Beaufort, it's wonderful to see you again. I've been trying to set up a meeting for a while now." I pushed my way into the room, greeting the mayor like we were the best of friends.

His eyes darted around as he very carefully pushed me back. I knew he was looking for an escape; I had him cornered, and there was very little he could do without seeming like a bit of a cad. He searched for a way to avoid talking to me, glancing from his office, to me, to his secretary. I could tell nothing was coming to him. That was when his shoulders dropped like the pole holding them up had been removed.

"What can I do for you, Miss Porter?" he asked.

"If I can have but a moment of your time. It won't take long, I promise. But it's best if we spoke alone."

"Of course. This way." He stepped aside so I could enter.

"First, I would love to know what Mr. Waring had on you—other than the affair with his wife."

"What do you mean?" Mr. Beaufort asked.

"I mean, what was he blackmailing you about? And what did he want from you?"

I sat in one of the two chairs facing the desk. I wanted him to know I was here until I decided it was time to leave.

"How do you know I was being blackmailed?" He swiped his hand through his hair as beads of sweat formed on his forehead.

"Because he tried to blackmail everyone. Why would you be an exception?"

"It was about the Mallorys. I wouldn't be in office without them, and sometimes they take advantage of that. But I would never do anything that would harm the town."

"Of course not. Did you pay the blackmailer?"

"I did. It was worth it just to get him to go away."

"Did he go away?" I leaned forward, intently interested in where this conversation was headed.

"He did for a while. Until he found out about the affair. He was livid."

"Do you know who any of his other victims were?"

"I assumed Mr. Farrows was one; that's why he was arrested."

"But the blackmail failed. Mr. Farrows didn't give in to Mr. Waring. They were at an impasse. Mr. Farrows is innocent of this and should be released. In fact, you have more of a motive to kill the man than Mr. Farrows."

"But then I don't have a suspect."

"You will, though. Release Mr. Farrows, and I will reveal everything I know at the musical tomorrow night."

*   *   *

Chapter Seventeen

New Lankersham, September 25, 1850

Dear Diary,

I'm still not sure about the mayor. He doesn't look like he's the type to kill a man, but really, does a murderer have a certain look? Or does it just come down to whether a person feels strongly enough about their need to dispose of a person? Mr. Waring seems like a person who was easy to dislike. I'm glad my interactions with him were quite limited. I would hate to be a suspect in another crime.

*   *   *   **

I arrived at our hotel room just in time to see Lia scurrying around. She was going from one place to the next with impressive speed and zero intentions. I couldn't help but laugh. It appeared that the bed had gotten the best of Lia again.

"Are you ready to go to Rika's?" I asked.

"Almost, I was a little late getting out of bed. Not that anyone is surprised by that." Lia looked around. "Have you seen my gloves?"

I looked down at the table next to me. "You mean these gloves?" I picked up a pair of white crocheted gloves and held them up.

Lia snatched them out of my hands. "Yes! I've been looking for these forever. I'm ready now."

I followed Lia out of our hotel room to the lift, then out the lobby doors. I let the doorman know a cab was required.

"Ah, Miss Porter," the concierge said.

I turned to see him running after Lia and me, waving a paper in his hand.

"Someone left a message for you."

"Thank you." I grabbed the missive, but before I could open it, the doorman was there holding a carriage for us. Before I took a seat, I stuffed the paper into my reticule. I would just have to look at it later.

"Did the mayor tell you anything?" Lia asked.

"What? . . . Ah yes, the mayor. Turns out, he was another victim of Mr. Waring's blackmail scheme, and it only got worse once the affair started."

"Do you think he killed Mr. Waring?" Lia grasped the seat as the cab hit something in the road that sent us careening across the seats. Someone should really come up with a way to make traveling smoother.

"He had motive and opportunity, so I don't feel like I can dismiss him. But he originally paid Mr. Waring to keep quiet. If he was willing to pay at the beginning, what changed that would make him kill the man? Unless the motive was to free Mrs. Waring from her husband. But even if that was it, unless they waited the two years it would take to finish mourning, it would have caused quite the scandal."

"It sounds like you want to dismiss him as a suspect, though."

"I do, but I need more evidence. Which is why you need to keep Rika occupied while I snoop."

The carriage came to a sudden halt.

"What? That's impossible. There's no way she's going to sit with me if you aren't in the room. Tell me what you are looking for, and I'll find it for you. It makes so much more sense to do it my way." Lia wrung her hands.

The two of us alighted from the carriage and made

our way to Rika's massive front door. Her stuffy butler opened the door and stepped aside to let us into the home with only a minor sniff.

"Darlings, I'm so happy to see you." Rika greeted us with an unusual amount of enthusiasm. "Especially you, Lia; I fear I owe you an apology for my behavior during the last time you visited. I hope you can forgive me." Rika took Lia by the arm and escorted us into the front parlor.

I sat in one of the many chairs in the room while Lia and Rika sat next to each other on a lovely velvet settee. Rika poured tea while Lia and I settled in. She then leaned back with a satisfied smile on her face.

"Honoria, you will never believe what happened this morning." Rika paused.

Lia leaned in. "What happened?"

"Apparently, Mayor Beaufort went down to the police station today and ordered them to release Mr. Farrows. He's going to be at the musicale tomorrow."

"That's wonderful. You must be so happy for your friend. Where is Mr. Rochester? I would love to talk to him about what he's going to be playing tomorrow. Is it something new?" I took a sip of my tea.

"He's not here right now. I believe he's rehearsing. He wants the music for tomorrow night to be a complete surprise. He's been gone for hours every day."

"Oh, how disappointing! I was really hoping to speak with him." I jostled the table, causing tea to spill on my ensemble. "How clumsy of me! If you'll excuse me for a moment, I need to clean myself up."

I stood, avoiding any eye contact with Lia. I could already tell she was holding back laughter, and if I looked at her, I might dissolve into a fit of giggles. Instead, I focused on Rika, who was so concerned I almost felt guilty.

"Of course, Honoria, please take your time. I hope you didn't burn yourself?" Concern laced her words, increasing my guilt.

"Thank you, I'll be back shortly." I scurried out of the room like I was going to the water closet. Instead, I tiptoed up the stairs to the room Rika had once said Mr. Rochester was staying in.

I shut the door behind me and leaned against it for a moment, determining my plan of attack. In the opposite corner was a desk with a few drawers. It seemed as good a place as any to start. Careful to disturb as little as possible, I looked through the papers. It appeared Mr. Rochester was composing something new. The writing on it looked like the composer was hesitant or unsure of himself. But Mr. Rochester was such a splendid success, why would he be concerned? That was all that was on the desk and in those drawers: unfinished sheet music.

The bedside tables also had drawers, so I made my way towards the grand bed and side tables. There I found more sheet music written in a different hand, one more authoritative. The music also looked livelier; although, I could barely play an instrument, so what did I really know? Nothing.

There has to be something else—wait, was the drawer front deeper than the drawer? I looked inside, and sure enough, a false bottom opened. A black leather journal was hidden in the compartment.

I picked it up, noticing the initials embossed on the front of the cover. I opened the book. The writing inside was strong, assertive even. In the journal was a list of names; I recognized a few, like Mr. Farrows, Ambrose, Mayor Beaufort, Mr. Mallory, and Mr. Rochester. There were even more names that I did not recognize. I read the entries next to the names that I recognized. There were mentions of railway sales, horse doping, voting fraud, and stolen musical works. There was even mention of a suspicious death related to one of the other crimes. I shoved the journal into my pocket and went back to tea.

*　　*　　*

Chapter Eighteen

New Lankersham, September 26, 1850

Dear Diary,

I've solved it. This morning, I spent a good amount of time alerting the authorities about my suspicions. Not that it did any good whatsoever. They all just looked at me like I belonged in an asylum. It got to the point that I was afraid to continue in case that's exactly where someone with a modicum of power in this town decided I should spend the rest of my days. I wasn't sure if the funds I've amassed would be enough to deter any of them. I did visit Mr. Farrows today and informed him of my plan for the evening. It is of the utmost importance someone knows what I am about to do.

*   *   *

I looked at my emerald silk dress in the mirror and tugged on the pouf sleeves, lowering the bodice on my shoulders. I grabbed one of my more elaborate necklaces, the stones a perfect match. The final touch was a dyed green feather that I pinned into my up-swept curls. The green complemented my hair perfectly. I put on my gloves, grabbed a cloak, and made my way to Lia's room.

"I'm ready, Honoria. I finally remembered what it's like to be on time." Lia rushed out of her room in a delightful ice-blue confection of a dress. She pulled on her gloves as she made her way to the lift. I trailed behind, amused at her definition of "on time."

I continued to follow Lia down the familiar halls to the lift and then down to the elegant lobby. The Standard felt like home, which made me itch to leave. I feared the comfort of this place was wearing out, and something or someone was going to be the catalyst that caused me, and by default, Lia, to pack our bags and move on to the next place. Wherever that next place was.

The ride to Rika's was uneventful. I was in my head about . . . well . . . everything. From the murder, to Mr.

Farrows, to why I felt this urge to move on to something or somewhere else. My mind felt like the wheels on the carriage, just spinning through all the different thoughts over and over again, but never stopping to fixate on one of them. That was until we came to a halt. It was time. The musical performance of Daniel Rochester awaited us.

Lia and I disembarked from the hackney to knock on the home's impressive doors. The supercilious butler answered with his usual sniff of disdain. I didn't know what I did to upset him so; it made me want to ask why the disapproval. It also made me wonder if he really disapproved or if he was just playing the part of a stuffy butler. I would ask, but I was sure that would only cause an even more disdainful sniff.

"Honoria, Lia! I'm so happy to see you again." Rika kissed each of us on the cheek. "I know, you're going to tell me you were here just yesterday. But that was yesterday and now it's today, and I've spent the day missing my friends while I prepared for tonight's event."

"That seems a bit excessive, Rika. I'm sure you were much too busy to give us even a passing thought." I took in the elegant decor. Tonight's theme seemed to be white and gold. A variety of white flowers in brushed gold vases sat around the room, and gold fabric swooped from the chandeliers to the outsides of the room. It was stunning in the evening light.

"I'm never too busy to miss my dear friends. Come, let's find you some seats near me for the musical." Rika made her way into the music room. "The mayor is already here, as are Mrs. Waring and the Mallorys, and of course, Ambrose is here. He was such a dear today helping me get all the last-minute details just right."

A loud knock on the door interrupted her progress. I heard the familiar disdainful sniff as I turned. There, in the doorway, was Mr. Farrows. My heart quickened as I looked at his rather well put-together frame. Behind me there was a gasp, followed by a shattering of glass. I turned to see Mrs. Waring standing in the door, mouth agape. Behind her, Mayor Beaufort leaned in towards Mrs. Waring, whispering something in her ear. Behind the mayor was Daniel Rochester, and at his feet were shards of crystal.

"I'm going to say hello to Mr. Farrows," I whispered to Lia. She nodded before making her way to the music room as I returned to the foyer.

Ambrose and Rika were already there, gushing over Mr. Farrows. It felt false to me. While they had done nothing to imply he was guilty, they also had done very little to help prove his innocence. The fickleness of high society was consistent wherever one was, and it left me feeling disheartened by those I called friends.

"Mr. Farrows, how nice to see you again. I feel like it has been ages." It had not been ages. I spoke to him this morning to ensure he showed up tonight.

"It has been too long since I've been blessed by your loveliness." He took my gloved hand, deftly popped the pearl button at my wrist, and placed a kiss right where my pulse fluttered. I took my hand back, trying to hide the unbuttoned glove from Rika and Ambrose.

"Honoria, I did not know you and Mr. Farrows were on such familiar terms?" Rika looked at me with a raised eyebrow.

"We became better acquainted as I tried to prove his innocence."

"Yes, dear Rika, if it wasn't for your friend here, I would surely be whiling away my time behind bars still. But she convinced the mayor of my innocence. I am forever in her debt." Mr. Farrows's smile took my breath away. He turned towards me and winked. "Shall we?" he asked with a proffered arm.

Rika was called back into the music room. Mr. Farrows and I followed until he pulled me into an alcove. He pressed my back up against the cold wall while his warmth engulfed the rest of me. I looked up to see him lower his mouth to mine. The warmth of his lips on mine was nice, but I knew there was more; I wanted more. My tongue darted out to lick his lower lip. His response was all that I could hope for. His hands roamed downward until I felt them scrunch up my skirt.

I pulled away from his embrace.

"Now is not the time," I said.

"It seemed like the perfect time a moment ago." He smirked. "We should go somewhere to finish what we started." He leaned in to nuzzle my neck, his trail of kisses sending a shiver up my spine.

I shimmied out of his embrace. "Maybe," I said with an arched eyebrow before gently pushing him out of my way. With a swish of my skirts, I entered the music room.

Chapter Nineteen

New Lankersham, September 26, 1850

Dear Diary,

I went from bored to intrigued in an instant, it would seem. I was ready to pack up and leave this town for something new and different until . . . well . . . Mr. Farrows was released from jail. Now, I'm reminiscing about that kiss. I could barely listen to the music, and when I did, it was nothing like what I had heard at the Opera House.

*   *   *

"Everyone, it's time to take a seat. Mr. Rochester is about to begin." It was clear Rika was thrilled about her accomplishment. It was quite the coup to have the conductor play in her home.

With one last glance over my shoulder at Mr. Farrows, I made my way to Lia's side. She looked at me with knowing eyes. In turn, I blushed what I was sure was an unbecoming shade of red. Lia just laughed and turned back to the front of the room, where Mr. Rochester stood behind a grand piano. He bowed to the crowd and flipped his tails as he sat on the bench.

The crowd took a collective breath, waiting for him to play. I wanted to hear something as whimsical and joyous as what I had heard before. Mr. Rochester's fingers caressed the piano keys as he played. I looked over at Lia, shocked at the depressing tones emanating from the piano. Lia's eyes were wide, her mouth agape. Her face was an expression of how I felt. Although, I shouldn't have been surprised since this just confirmed one of my theories.

The music continued. Everyone in the crowd shifted in their seats, looking at those closest to them in wonder. Not the wonder produced by Rochester's other pieces; instead, it was disbelief that the same person who wrote music renowned for its joy could also have composed the piece being played right now. If only they knew what Mr. Waring had known: that the composers were not the same person.

I watched as Mr. Rochester ended the piece with a

flourish, looking up with expectation in his eyes. The silence in the room was palpable. I clapped to break the tension, at least for the moment. The rest of the room followed my lead. Mr. Rochester bowed as if the delay in applause was because of our amazement, not our disappointment.

"It's time," I whispered to Lia as I stood. I searched the room for Mr. Farrows, nodding towards the library when our eyes met.

Lia moved to gather Rika and Ambrose, escorting them to the library. I approached Mr. Rochester, but my eyes followed Mr. Farrows as he found Mayor Beaufort and the others, and retired to the library.

"Mr. Rochester, I did not know you had such a range with your music. Tonight's performance was . . . unexpected," I said, taking him by the arm.

"I have always wanted to show off the diversity of my skills. It was wonderful to share this with such an intimate group." He puffed out his chest as I surreptitiously pulled him towards the library. "Excuse me, where are we going?"

"I was hoping to show you something in the library. You see, I came across this journal the other day, and I was curious if you knew anything about it?" I carefully pulled the journal out of my reticule, the embossed letters *WW* clearly visible.

He grabbed the book from my hand and shoved it in his pocket. "Where did you get this?" he asked through clenched teeth. He dragged me towards the library. I assumed he thought I was taking him to an empty room, but I was smarter than he thought.

"I think the better question is, what were you doing with Mr. Waring's journal? Or perhaps I should call it his blackmail book," I said as he pushed the doors open to find every potential suspect to Mr. Waring's murder staring at us.

Reece took a step forward, but I shook my head no. I did not need saving, at least not yet. Mr. Rochester dropped my arm as he looked around the room. All eyes were on him.

"You see, Mr. Rochester, despite having overheard the argument between Mr. Waring and Mr. Farrows with my own ears, it never made sense for Mr. Farrows to murder Mr. Waring. He didn't benefit from Mr. Waring's demise. So, I decided to do a little digging." I moved away from Mr. Rochester, walking from person to person. "I discovered some interesting things about this city and the people in it. Like the fact that there are people willing to drug horses to win races. Ambrose was accused of that, but anyone who's seen him with his horses would know that was an impossibility.

"Then there are the political shenanigans. For a country so proud of their elections, the ballot box stuffing in this city is intolerable. Not to mention how easy it is to buy off politicians. It turns out Mr. Waring knew about that as well, but Mayor Beaufort agreed to pay Mr. Waring's price, and the Mallorys—well, they're a fickle lot. Instead of paying Mr. Waring, they intended to back him in the next election. Sorry, Mayor. Then you have poor Mrs. Waring. Her husband was not kind, and she found solace elsewhere. Mayor Beaufort paid for that as well."

Mr. Rochester's eyes followed me around the room. He took in each and every word that I said, barely breathing because he knew what was coming.

"The truly interesting tale that Mr. Waring uncovered was one of a young composer and his secretary. The composer was struggling to make it because the world found his music too dark, too depressing. But his secretary wrote the most beautiful, might I even say, whimsical pieces. That's what you're known for, isn't it, Mr. Rochester?" I paused, not expecting an answer. "See, the secretary was madly in love with the composer and would do anything for him, including letting him put his name on the secretary's creations. That is, until the secretary discovered the composer would never love him. The secretary threatened to expose him, ruining everything the composer had built, leaving him no choice. The composer killed his secretary. At least, that's what Mr. Waring wrote about. But he never got a payment from the composer. Instead, the composer set up an outing to the races. He made sure everyone around had a reason to want to dispose of Mr. Waring. And in the stable, the composer bludgeoned Mr. Waring, leaving him to die but taking a small journal. The journal, or blackmail book, you have in your pocket right now, Mr. Rochester."

Daniel Rochester looked like a cornered animal. His eyes darted from person to person until they came to rest on me.

"Why is everyone out to ruin my life?" He grabbed me with one arm, pressing a knife to my throat with the other.

"Mr. Rochester, why don't we sit and talk, find a solution to this little conundrum." Rika moved forward.

"Don't come any closer." Mr. Rochester pointed the knife at Rika.

I grabbed the feathered hairpin and stabbed the arm holding me, then stomped on his foot as hard as I could. The knife clattered to the ground. Mr. Farrows pulled me away from Mr. Rochester and wrapped his arms around my waist.

"I'll have a deputy take care of him immediately,"

Mayor Beaufort said.

* * *

Chapter Twenty

New Lankersham, September 30, 1850

Dear Diary,

I can't believe I solved the murder. Now everything can go back to normal. Although, I'm not sure I want to go back to normal, whatever that is. Over the last few days, Lia and I fell into a rhythm. One that often involved Mr. Farrows. It was nice, it was comfortable, it was even exciting at times. But, every now and then this urge to move on would overcome me. It felt like a necessity to move on and see something new.

*   *   *

The morning sun filtered through the windows as I stretched. I smiled as my arm brushed up against a warm body. Reece rolled towards me and nuzzled my neck, causing me to giggle.

A knock on the door interrupted our playful moment.

"Honoria, are you awake?" Lia called through the door.

"Reece, get out of bed, hurry," I whispered as I leapt out of bed. I scrambled around the room to find his clothes, throwing each piece at him as I found it. "Out the window you go." I pushed him onto the balcony, taking a moment to enjoy the view of him putting on his shirt before I closed the drapes. I threw on my dressing gown before answering the door.

"Good morning, Lia," I said somewhat breathless.

Lia pushed her way into the room. "You can come in off the balcony, Mr. Farrows. I know you're out there." She pushed the curtains back.

"Thank you, Lia." Reece stepped back into the room.

"I was preparing our things for laundry and found this in your reticule. It's the letter that came the day before the musicale." Lia held out a crumpled piece of paper.

"I completely forgot about the letter." I grabbed it from her and sat at my vanity. Smoothing it out, I read who it was from. "I wasn't expecting to hear from him again. The captain sent us this."

"Captain? Who is this captain?" A note of jealousy tinged Reece's tone.

"Captain Castleberry; he was the captain on our voyage over," I said, my attention focused on the letter.

My brow furrowed as I read. I don't know what I expected to be in the letter, especially since I didn't think I would ever hear from the captain again. Instead, he took the time to write me, to warn me.

Lia stood, wringing her hands, something she hadn't done in a long time. "What is it, Honoria? You look like you've seen a ghost."

I stood and paced around the room. "They've found me, or at least they are close to finding me."

"Who's found you?" Reece asked, bewildered.

Lia jumped up and started organizing my things for packing. "They haven't found you yet. If we go somewhere else tonight, they won't find us anytime soon. I'll have the hotel staff bring our trunks up right away."

"Who's found you and why are you running?" Reece persisted, even though Lia and I were both ignoring him.

"What exactly did the captain say?" Lia stopped moving.

"What . . . Oh, let me see." I sat down. "He says an investigator from Brythion was going from ship to ship asking about me. He approached Captain Castleberry, but he pretended he had never heard of me. Subterfuge will only last so long when it comes to my family. They will figure it out. At least, my mother will keep going until she finds me and marries me off to someone of her choice. She's tried to trap me before; she'll do it again."

"Deep breaths, Honoria. You didn't panic this much when you were almost trapped the first time. We just need to slow down and think," Lia said.

"I had a plan before, but I've been complacent. In all honesty, I never thought anyone would come looking for me."

"Ahem . . . I believe you are forgetting that there's someone in this room who might be able to help." Reece stood, drawing my eyes to him, reminding me he was here.

"I'm sorry, I forgot you were here," I said.

"That much was obvious."

"I'm sorry, Reece. This letter was a shock, to say the least."

"I could tell." He walked behind me and rubbed my shoulders. "You did so much for me; the least I could do is help you escape this investigator. If that's truly what you want?"

Glancing up at Reece, I'm sure there were stars in my

eyes. I knew I could rescue myself, but there was something about him offering to rescue me that made me feel quite fluttery.

"And how would you do that?" Lia interrupted the moment Reece and I were having.

"I do own a railroad. It's the fastest transportation out of town. I'd be more than happy to escort you at least part of the way," he said.

"That could really help, especially if the investigator is looking for women traveling together." Lia placed her hands on her skirt.

"It's an idea. But my family is not your concern. I wouldn't want you to go out of your way." It would be nice to have the help, but it felt wrong to accept help even if it made my heart flip-flop.

"It's not out of my way; I was already hoping you would let me do something to thank you. I've already put a few shares of my railroad in your name. It isn't much, but I thought it would help you out on your journey. It didn't seem like enough though. But getting you on a train to somewhere is something I can definitely do to help."

"If you're sure. When do you think we could leave?" My mind switched to planning mode. I needed to write a letter to Gwendolyn's family to thank them for the free hotel suite. It would be nice to say goodbye to Rika before moving on to a new place; who knows if I will see her again.

A knock on the door stopped all thoughts of planning my escape. What if I was already too late. Eyes wide, I looked from the door to Lia. It was impossible to breath while someone stood on the other side of the door and I didn't know who it was.

"Do you want me to answer?" Lia whispered.

A second knock pierced the quiet of the room. "Miss Porter… You have a delivery."

I nodded towards the door and whispered, "Lia, answer the door."

"Are you sure that's a good idea?" She hissed.

"No but what else can we do?" I answered through my teeth.

Instead, Reece, now fully dressed opened the door. He tipped the delivery boy and brought the package into the room. The package itself was huge. In fact it looked like a painting. Oh my, it was a painting.

"Are you going to open it?" Reece asked.

I glanced over at Lia, who was doing everything in her power not to laugh. "I would rather not."

"You should Honoria, you went through so much to get this painting." Lia giggled.

"Fine." I walked over to the brown paper wrapped package. Slowly untied the string, then removed the paper. Beneath the paper was an oil painting of me, languishing on a settee in my undergarments.

Reece looked at me, the painting, back at me. He raised an eyebrow. "It's really quite lovely. Remarkable, even."

"You should have it, as a reminder of the day we met." I was ready to return to the subject of my escape. "How long until you will be ready to leave."

"It would be best if I had two days to make the arrangements. It will ensure that there will be sleeper cars available, maybe even a private dining car." Reece pushed his hair back, deep in thought.

"That will be perfect because it gives me time to say goodbye to Rika."

*   *   *

Rika's stuffy butler sniffed his last judgmental sniff directed to Lia and me. I was going to miss coming here for tea and other events. But it turned out I was feeling restless for a reason, and I feared if I didn't leave, my adventures would be over.

"Honoria, Lia, it's wonderful to see you!" She kissed both of our cheeks. "I am a bit surprised. I don't think we had anything planned."

"We didn't have anything planned. But I wanted to come and say goodbye. Lia and I are leaving tomorrow," I said embracing my dear friend.

"What, you're leaving? Why?" Rika took my arm and then Lia's.

"I wasn't planning on it, at least not this soon. But it's become a necessity."

"Do you know where you are going?"

Lia and I looked at each other. We would be on a train tomorrow, and I did not know where to go.

"Not yet. Any suggestions?"

"Well, if you visited Gaofar, you could stay at my family's townhouse."

"It looks like we are headed to Gaofar." I glanced over at Lia, wondering if she remembered who else was traveling to Gaofar.

The three of us chatted for a bit until the carriage Reece sent for us arrived.

*　　*　　*

The three of us stood by the tracks waiting for the next train. I glanced around, my eyes darting from one person to another, wary of anyone who glanced our way. Lia stood beside me, staring straight ahead with her hands clasped in front of her. Every now and then I would see her wring her hands, a clear sign she was just as nervous as I was.

"If you two don't relax, people are going to wonder if I'm kidnapping you," Reece whispered in my ear. His breath sent tingles down my spine.

A quick glance up showed him looking at me, his eyes filled with concern. His concern almost calmed me. My fear, as real as it was for me, wouldn't be understood by many. In my head I could hear my sister's voice, filled with derision, asking what was so scary about marrying a handsome duke. Or my mother saying I was running away from every girl's dream. They didn't understand that it wasn't my dream, that it led to a future I didn't want at all. But my mother and sister weren't here. . . yet. Instead, I was standing next to two people who understood me, who were literally by my side.

I laughed as the train pulled into the station. Linking my arms through theirs, we boarded the train. I was ready for the next adventure, whatever it was.

*   *   *

Acknowledgements

Thank you to my friends and family for constantly supporting me on my author journey. I couldn't do this without you.

About Author

Stephanie K Clemens is known for many things: an author, photographer, dog mom, instagrammer, adventurer, teacher, lawyer, and more. When she's not sitting behind her laptop she can be found on some adventure. Most of the time it's a road trip with her two doggos, but recently it has been in the pages of a book.

Also By

Ladies of WACK Series

A Study in Steam

A Practicum in Perjury

A History in Horticulture – Coming Soon

Wynterfell Romances

For the Love of Hot Cocoa – Coming Soon

Novellas

The Adventures of Alex Granger

Kindle Vella

For the Love of Hot Cocoa

Stripped Away

The Adventures of Alex Granger

The Daring Adventures of Honoria Porter: Part 1

The Daring Adventures of Honoria Porter: Part 2

Practicum in Perjury

Children's Books written by S,K. Clemens

Frankie Wants to be a Sled Dog

www.ingramcontent.com/pod-product-compliance
Lightning Source LLC
Chambersburg PA
CBHW071337020826
48982CB00027B/1534/J